Urban Coyote

New Territory

**Michele Genest, Dianne Homan &
Jenny Charchun, Editors**

THE YUKON PUBLISHERS

Whitehorse

An earlier version of *I Like To Wear Dresses* by Ivan E. Coyote appeared in *Xtra West*. *Yellowlegs* by Al Pope was read on Richardson's Roundup on CBC Radio.

Published by Lost Moose Publishing, 58 Kluane Cres., Whitehorse, Yukon, Canada Y1A 3G7, phone 867-668-5076 or 668-3441, fax 867-456-4355, e-mail lmoose@yknet.ca

National Library of Canada cataloguing in publication data

Main entry under title :

Urban Coyote : new territory

ISBN 1-896758-09-6

1. Yukon Territory — Literary collections. 2. Canadian literature (English) — Yukon Territory. I. Genest, Michele. II. Homan, Dianne. III. Charchun, Jenny.

PS8255.Y8U72 2003   C810.8'09719'1   C2003-980207-8

Printed and bound in Canada

Cover photograph © Steve Brewis

The Urban Coyote Artists Collective and Lost Moose Publishing wish to gratefully acknowledge a contribution from the Government of Yukon Arts Fund and the Canada Council, which made publication of this volume possible.

Future submissions are invited. Contact the Urban Coyote Collective at 710 Strickland Street, Whitehorse, Yukon, Y1A 2K8.

Contents

ACKNOWLEDGEMENTS

The editors wish to thank Reinhard Saure,
Adam Green, Michael Reynolds and Syth Charchun.
Special thanks to consulting editor Patricia Sanders.

Introduction

Wayne Grady

THE FOUR MONTHS I spent in the Yukon in 2001-2002,
even though two of them (November and February) were
winter months, were hardly enough to confer sourdough
status upon me, alas, but they did give me a wonderful
opportunity to become acquainted with a vibrant and
dedicated literary community. As Writer-in-Residence at
the Whitehorse Public Library, I met and talked with dozens
of writers from all over the Yukon, read and discussed their
work, attended numerous readings and workshops, and
witnessed a kind of northern renaissance in the launching of
the first *Urban Coyote* as well as of a new literary magazine,
Out of Service, and a small publishing house, Patricia
Robertson's Linnaea Press. It was an exciting time to be in
the Yukon, and the headiness of it is still with me.

That headiness is also, as the appearance of *Urban
Coyote, New Territory* attests, still with a great many Yukon

writers. There is, here, a fine outpouring of writing from the Yukon community. That that community is growing is indicated by the fact that only four of the 17 writers included here — Al Pope, Dean Eyre, Michael Reynolds and Yvette Nolan — were also in the first *Urban Coyote*, and nearly all the rest are published here for the first or second time in their writing careers. All the work in this volume exudes more confidence and sophistication than is commonly found in a collection of new voices from a "new territory."

What first struck me in reading this anthology were the links it contains with the larger community of Canadian writers, for here are many of the images and themes that have been dominant in Canadian literature for nearly 200 years. Canadian writers have long been at pains to establish their work as unique expressions of their own landscapes and experiences, and yet at the same time eager to show that they are part of a larger tradition of English or French literature. I sense the same dual forces at work in this collection: here are writers who, with their own individual voices, are writing about the unique power and beauty of the Yukon, and at the same time are very consciously taking their places within a larger literary tradition that includes everyone who has written about the harsh Canadian land and the ways we have found to survive with it.

Indeed, the land is one of the chief recurring figures in these stories and poems, almost a character in itself (as the Heath often is in Thomas Hardy, or the Prairie in Sinclair Ross). In the first story, Graham McDonald's *Tough Sledding*, the land is a mute, implacable force that is simply there, and Katie must either deal with it or not, on its own terms. In the south, people have changed the land to suit their own purposes; in the north it's the other way around. Although people come to the north for various reasons of their own — as miners (the father of Katie's baby, or the absent miners in Brenda Schmidt's *Life After Mining*), foresters (as in Dean Eyre's *The Surprising Weight of the Fall*), or out of a vague sense of adventure (Philip Adams' *Crow Jane* or Yvette Nolan's *Rented Room*) — in the end the land remains unchanged; it is the people who alter to accommodate it, or else they leave. *Life After Mining* isn't so much about mining as it is "about light and where you'll go/when the place shuts down, is done with you —"

A surprising number of those people leave — usually the men, I have noticed. The single woman is the other recurring image that runs through these stories and poems — McDonald's Katie, Nolan's Angela, Liz Gontard's Martha, Al Pope's Irene, and Patti Fraser's unnamed central character — the abandoned woman who finds new strength, a determined selfhood, in her abandonment. Although this theme runs all through Canadian literature, from Susanna Moodie to Richard Wright, it is particularly strong in Yukon writing, as I had noticed it in the current of Yukon life. The powerful, lone, female figure, not conquering her environment (conquering is a male conceit, which explains why the men left) but coming to terms with it, often with a baby on her hip to symbolize the future.

Not all of these pieces adhere to themes of the land; many of them could have been written anywhere. Tory Russell's *Final Move* is about how we die, not necessarily by freezing in the bush; Jerome Stueart, represented here with a story and two poems, writes with deep feeling about the forces at work in the human heart; and Ivan E. Coyote deals with a different kind of otherness. But these works are imbued with an unmistakable northernicity, are informed by a connection with nature, human and wild, that rings with authenticity. It is no accident that they were written where they were.

Erling Friis-Baastad once told me that when he alighted from the bus in Whitehorse two decades ago he felt as though he had landed in a poetic wasteland, himself an exiled Ovid in a land that had yet to be adequately described. Clearly he is no longer that lone figure. As I discovered during my brief sojourn two years ago, and as this anthology proves, there is now a chorus of voices coming from the land. "We are learning to bend close/" Erling wrote in the first volume of *Urban Coyote*, "and reach down to these;/ logs, sticks, even boards ..." There is much power and insight in his "we." This anthology, grounded as it is in the Yukon and its people, is a testament to the lessons that have been learned. To borrow from Brenda Schmidt's stunning poem, *Words to Another Forest Song*:

"Here is the whole composition, its elements
wild notes struck ..."

Wayne Grady
Athens, Ontario
June, 2003

Tough Sledding

Graham McDonald

ON THIS EARLY morning, in the season of long nights, Katie's eyes close and she imagines herself floating above the tent frame, above the clearing in the pine forest south of Whitehorse. In moonlight the white canvas shimmers above the snow and the orange plastic tarp pulled over the ridgepole ripples in a late November breeze. Smoke tears away from the chimney top. A slide of snow from the roof startles one of the sled dogs staked out north of the tent frame where their plywood houses sit in packed circles of snow. South of the dog yard and the drive that loops around the tent frame, snow is settled on the edges of the house foundation and on the shed, on piles of building materials and Phil's 4x4. Near the tent frame, heavy frost covers both a rusted Toyota pickup and a dog sled that points towards two large aspens, the gateposts of Katie's training trail.

Inside, the airtight stove pumps heat and the sleeping loft is muggy with kerosene vapours and woodsmoke. Katie started the fire half an hour earlier, put on the kettle and added meal to the dog bucket for the watering she'll do when the day starts to brighten around nine. Suddenly too hot, she tosses back the covers and strips Jeremy so his bottom can air. He's big for six months. It was all she could do to keep running the dogs — over the protests of her doctor — until the end of the snow in March. Jeremy was born the second of May, all nine pounds six ounces of him.

She leans over the edge of the loft to drop the diaper into the soaking-bucket behind the ladder. The tent frame is compact: her own design. There are shelves of bottles and jars that glint in the lamplight, a counter, a sink and a propane hotplate. In the corner under the loft there is a brown chair with flat armrests where she eats most of her meals. The walls behind and beside it are lined with Canadian, American and British novels, history and how-to books. Katie can still see flashes of fire from the draught on the airtight so she lies back with a contented sigh. Jeremy finds her breast and sucks softly, still half asleep. Flickers of light lick at the canvas ceiling and she drifts.

Katie has lived in the tent frame almost a year and a half, as long as she's had her dogs. This is her second winter on Phil's lot, her third in the Yukon running a team. The first winter she handled for a musher named Frank and helped him out with training. In late February that first winter, she made a night run that hooked her on running dogs.

The team had climbed bars of light and shade thrown by the moon through a strip of trees to Katie's right. She and the dogs, raced by their shadows, headed uphill, clinging to a Cat track on the side of a forested valley that fell away into the M'Clintock River. The dogs pulled hard and the tuglines thrummed, whispering the sled through the snow. Each breath felt like pure oxygen. She called a "Haw" and Copper, her lead dog, turned the team left onto a moon-bright trail that moved away from the river and climbed above treeline. Their shadow shot ahead, an arrow, and Katie ran the steep pitches, clinging to the driving bow, feet pounding between the runner tails, the neck of her parka open and the hood thrown back.

Copper's ears pricked up and she whooped when the trail opened onto an alpine valley. It stretched along a creek marked by snow-humped willows and glassy overflow. Glittering slopes, studded by shadowed rock and triangles of balsam fir, spread towards peaks that glowed in moonlight.

When she tilted over the lip of that valley, her world came into focus. She halted the team and ran up to hug Copper, her chest bursting — as if she had inhaled all the joy of winter in one breath.

At the end of the season, Frank gave her Copper. "He must really like you," he said. "He never worked for me like that." Frank blushed when Katie hugged him and planted a kiss on his cheek.

THE KETTLE ERUPTS, and a splash of water pops and hisses on the stove-top. Katie turns from Jeremy, banks a pillow against him and drops down the ladder. The floor is cold through her sock feet. She pours steaming water from the kettle into the enamel basin beside the lamp.

When she climbs back to the loft, with change stuff and a hot washcloth, Jeremy gurgles awake. She kneels beside him, washes his bottom, slips a diaper on and pins it snug. Jeremy coos as she buzzes her lips on his belly. "You're my man, Jeremy. Let's get this show on the road." She slips plastic pants over the diaper and gives the waistband a gentle snap. "It's a new day."

Katie runs her dogs every day, anywhere from twelve to twenty miles — and still longer runs later in the season. Today she plans a twenty-miler: twelve miles on the northeast loop down towards the river and then another eight-mile loop west of the lot, half of it in the ditch along the highway. If Jeremy fusses she can cut the run short at the end of the first loop, after the climb up from the river, and just take the trail into the back of the lot. Her goal is to get a thousand miles on the dogs before March, when she'll run the Percy deWolfe race from Dawson City to Eagle, Alaska, and back.

She stirs the porridge and peers out through the canvas flap while Jeremy bangs a spoon on his highchair tray. In the yard, Copper's ears perk at the morning sounds. He lifts one leg at a time over the sill of his house, plants his paws in the snow and stretches. He sniffs the yellow-iced corner of his doghouse, lifts his leg to contribute and then jumps on top to shake himself. The slap of chain against plywood sets the rest of the yard barking. The tan patches over Copper's eyes lift and he stares at the tent frame. Katie feels the corners of her own eyes crinkle in response.

Phil had let Katie build the tent frame on his lot not long after they met, a year ago spring, a year before Jeremy.

"I won't be building anything permanent for a while yet," he told her. "You can hang here for as long as you like." She built the floor and wall in sections, so she could move it later if she had to.

Phil worked as a diamond driller and spent most of his time in the bush. "Packing away money," he told her. He had started stashing building materials on the property for an eventual house. He said it would make sense to have someone living on the lot so things didn't disappear.

Over the course of that summer he took to dropping by when he was in town, sometimes to drop off salvaged windows or doors, other times just to visit. There'd be the rumble of his 4x4 pulling up to the tent, a tap on the plywood and then a soft, "Hey — may I come in?" It always happened like that, without notice, always the "may," as if he didn't take her friendship for granted. Other days there'd just be a new pile of scavenged building materials in the yard, and she wouldn't even see him.

Then, some time towards the end of summer, he stayed a night — only after she made him drive to town for condoms. Later, during her slide into sleep, when she was spooned in front of him, his tears dampened the nape of her neck. Feeling closer to him then than during their lovemaking, she asked, "What's the matter?"

"I'm just sad," he said.

She turned to him and traced the tears with her finger. "Why?"

"Just 'cause," he sighed. "Things you can't change. Don't worry."

She pulled him to her, they made love again, and then she lay in silence until his breathing deepened. The next day he was gone.

KATIE FEELS THE blast of noise — barks and howls — as she struggles out of the tent frame with the stained feed bucket. A splash darkens the leg of her faded overalls. Her parka is ballooned in front by Jeremy in his Snugli.

"Hush!" The dogs quiet and pace on the arcs of their chains. She knows that the silence will hold only until she dishes up the first feed.

Last winter, from October up until Christmas, she had retched her way through this routine. The fishy smell of the feed made her gag every time. She was working an early shift at the café at the Carcross cut-off, running a heavy training schedule with the dogs, and she crashed into bed every night. It was only after she'd missed two periods that she even let herself think she could be pregnant. They'd used condoms, hadn't they? She hadn't thought of herself as being in a relationship; she wasn't sleeping with Phil regularly. Hell, she barely saw him.

"You're near the end of your first trimester," Dr. Helmsford told her. "You need to make some decisions." When he said that, she realized that she'd been talking to Jeremy for weeks — she was sure he was a boy — in the same unconscious way she talked to the dogs when she did her chores.

"WHERE'S YOUR BOWL?" she asks Copper, nudging him with her knee. Copper stretches a paw under his house. Katie holds the back of Jeremy's head with her hand and gets down on her knees to dig Copper's bowl out. Then she stands and drops it in front of the dog. "Copper," she says, "some day I'm not going to feed you if you don't have your dish." She uses a stainless steel dipper bolted to the end of a piece of willow to serve up his ration. When everyone has their feed, the only sounds in the dog yard will be slurps and chain clangs against metal bowls.

Katie had told Phil she was pregnant in late October when he was down from Dawson, a week after she'd seen the doctor. They had just made love, she felt warm and cared for, and so she told him. Right away he started talking about an abortion. Katie pushed him away from her, into the tight angle between the canvas ceiling and the shelf at the edge of the mattress. "He's not an it," she pointed to her belly and her eyes boiled with tears. "He's our baby."

"How do I know that?" Phil loomed over her like a spider as he tried to get to the ladder. She slapped him. His face tightened and he hovered an instant. Then he swung over the edge of the loft and dropped heavily to the floor. He left without saying another word.

The following Tuesday morning, in the middle of the breakfast rush, he called the café from Dawson. She was clearing a table, piling plates and cups into the grey plastic bussing tray. "It's your sweetie," Yvonne called from the door of the kitchen, as she held up the telephone receiver. Katie wiped the table with tight, deliberate swirls while conversation and cigarette smoke eddied around her. "Katie?" Yvonne was beside her, tucking a strand of grey, frizzy hair behind her ear. "It sounds like he really needs to talk to you."

Katie set the tray on the counter, brushed her hands against her apron and went to the phone.

"Hi," she said.

"I thought we should talk." Phil sounded subdued.

"So talk."

"I'm not near a phone much."

"I know."

"Well … you surprised me the other night.…" He paused.

"This wasn't part of my plan either."

"Yeah — I know you want to race the dogs."

"Uh-huh." Katie turned her back away from the cash register and faced into the kitchen, her head bent over the phone. Yvonne rang up the breakfast bills for two guys who worked at the salvage yard across the way.

"Look," Phil was saying, "I'm not ready to be a father."

Katie watched the griddle as the whites of a pair of eggs bubbled and browned on the edges.

"Even if the baby is mine, it's not up to me to tell you what to do," Phil said.

She squeezed her eyes shut and leaned against the wall.

"I want you to know that you can keep the tent frame on the lot for as long as you want … and if I can help out.…"

Katie felt a wave of nausea. She dropped the phone. "Yvonne," she said, "your eggs are burning." Then she rushed to the washroom.

KATIE DOES ANOTHER round of the yard with shovel and pail after she's finished the dog watering. This time the dogs are focused on her. Rickie, a young leader, puts paws up on the front of her parka and Jeremy giggles at the scratching against his back. "Off," Katie says. Rickie drops and then leaps on top of her house for face-to-face attention. Katie scratches her behind the ears and accepts chin licks.

Anger had overcome pride some time in November and she had tried to reach Phil several times, leaving word with the drilling company that she would like him to call. On her fourth attempt, the secretary in the office assured her again that she had relayed each of the previous messages. Then her voice dropped and softened and she said, "You know, Phil has a friend in Dawson — a woman he's been seeing for a couple of years. I thought you should know." Katie massages the back of her neck, remembers the summer lovemaking and the scald of Phil's tears.

KATIE SCRAPES UP the frozen turds in Copper's circle and thumps them into the black plastic bucket. "You going to be all right to run today?" she asks. He prances on his house-top. She strips her mitts, doctors a web crack between the pads on his left front paw and then slips on a new bootie. "You'll be fine," she says. Mitts back on, she bangs her hands together and heads to the tent frame. Speaking down her parka front to Jeremy, she says, "Let's put some wood in the stove and get warmed up, then we'll go for our run."

By last December her clothes weren't fitting but the morning sickness was gone. She hadn't told her family in Mississauga that she was pregnant and planning to have her baby. They wanted her to come home for Christmas and again offered to send airfare, but she didn't want to break the training routine she had going. She couldn't figure out how to tell them that, so she just said she couldn't find anyone to look after the dogs. Her mom sent one of her Christmas cakes.

On solstice night, Katie had taken the dogs on the second loop of the trail — the first time in the dark. The team was excited by the blackness, the flash of her headlamp on the trees and a hard, fast trail. There was no holding the yearlings back. The turn at the highway right-of-way came too soon. She called the "Haw" too late. Copper hesitated, but Rickie and the young dogs kept going over the snowbank and onto the highway.

The team raced down the black pavement towards the moon. The screeching brake and shouted commands didn't slow them. She dragged her left foot, forcing the sled towards the shoulder. Then she threw it on its side and herself on top. Finally they stopped. She half-set the snowhook, dragged herself up the gangline, grabbed the leaders and hauled them over the snowbank. She hugged Copper and Rickie as a semi whined past swirling snow and grit over her and the team.

THE TENT FRAME has cooled down and there are only coals left in the bottom of the stove. She tumbles in some kindling and short logs, closes the lid, puts the kettle on top and opens the draught. In a few minutes it's puffing away and the kettle starts to steam. She pours a cup of hot water for herself, frees Jeremy from the Snugli and settles into the armchair, still wearing her parka and bunny boots. Jeremy nurses through her open shirt while she makes notes in her dog journal. Then she shifts Jeremy to her other breast and lets her head drop back.

Phil had showed up again in late April, the drilling contract done. She was so pregnant by then she was ready to burst and hadn't worked at the café for a week. "I want to be there for the birth," Phil told her. "I guess I should be there."

He said he'd pitch a tent of his own on the lot and help her look after the dogs until she could get rolling again. She felt too heavy with all she had to do to protest. "What about your woman in Dawson?" she had wanted to ask, but when he opened his arms, she had folded into him.

Phil was in the delivery room with her. When the nurse tucked Jeremy in beside her and Katie guided his mouth to her nipple, Dr. Helmsford said, "He's going to have red hair, just like his father." Phil beamed at both of them.

"Guess I'd better get going on the house," he said a couple of days later when she was back home. "Maybe we should move you two into a trailer in town for a while." She didn't know what to make of his building plans and she didn't like the trailer idea at all.

She did know that the dogs had all been pretty dry and several looked skinny even though he'd tended them for only a few days. "I'm sorry," she whispered to Copper. She wasn't going to leave them with Phil. She decided it wouldn't be much different working around the dogs with Jeremy in a Snugli than it had been when she was pregnant.

Phil bought a generator and chop saw, built a storage shed, and hired a backhoe and Cat to clear the building site and do ground work for the foundation and septic field. Then he started on the treated wood foundation. He got underway with energy most mornings, but petered out in the afternoons. Katie was sharing meals with him, but she wouldn't let him sleep with her every night. Sometimes, if she shrugged him away when he tried to cuddle, he would head for the cut-off where he'd buy off-sales. He was never out of beer. She noticed that if he had a beer with lunch, he'd be finished the case by dinnertime.

In early June, Phil told her that he'd have the house framed by mid-August. "Then by winter we'll have it closed in and you'll have a bathtub and flush toilet," he continued. Until then, she'd be hauling diaper pails to the laundromat and showering in town. All the water for both them and the dogs would still have to be carted from the cut-off in five-gallon plastic barrels.

A week later, with just the foundation complete and the septic field installed, he suddenly announced that he had to go up to Dawson for a week. When he came back he told her the drilling company had offered him good money for three months of wrestling pipe and pulling core on a mountaintop in South America. "Then we'll have enough saved so we can really give her shit this fall," he told her. The "we" was new, and it was the second time he'd said he'd be coming back. But the sudden change of plans? She wavered — maybe he'd settled things in Dawson.

"I know you want to race. This winter I can do the finishing work on the house and look after Jeremy. You'll be able to run the dogs every day." She hugged him when he said that. They set up a joint bank account before he left.

In August he left a phone message at the café to say that the contract was extended and that he'd be gone for at least another month. Then the bimonthly deposits to their account stopped.

"He hasn't returned from leave," the secretary told her in September. In October she put Katie straight through to the manager. He was blunt. "We can't pay him if he's not working. He's gone on benders before. We're not a babysitting service."

She gave away the pups she had trained over the summer. With what was left in the bank, she couldn't feed dogs that wouldn't pull in the team for another year. If she went back to work at the café, most of what she made would go to childcare and she'd wouldn't have enough time for the dogs.

KATIE SLAMS A last piece of wood into the stove, shoves it down with the lid and sets a rock on top of that. She gives Jeremy a quick diaper change, slides him into his red snowsuit and winds a knit scarf around his head. Then she sets him in the car seat she brought in from the truck. She closes the draught and stovepipe damper and carries him outside.

With all the training she's done, hookups are smooth. But they're never quiet. Jeremy howls with the dogs while she rocks the sled from side to side to free the runners, brushes off the sled bag and then sets the snowhook with the heel of her boot. Before she loads Jeremy, she ties the gee-line off to a stump for safety. She wraps a sleeping bag around both Jeremy and the car seat and settles the whole bundle in on top of the bags of feed she's got in the sled for weight. Jeremy's place is at the back of the sled bag, within easy reach, just in front of her place on the runners. The driving bow she holds onto when they're underway will act as a roll bar if the sled tips. Nestled in the bag, Jeremy calms. Katie snugs the sled-bag straps down on the car seat to hold it in place. She leaves an open flap at the top of the bag, so they can see each other, and pulls his scarf up over his nose. "Peek-a-boo!" she says, closing the flap and opening it again. Jeremy giggles and waggles his head side to side. He usually falls asleep as soon as they're moving.

The dogs wail and strain against their chains as she harnesses them. She hooks up Rickie and Copper first, side by side, and they lean into their harnesses, tugging on the long, centre gangline. She hooks the other dogs in pairs behind the leaders. Finally Katie clips the last dog into wheel position and pulls her mitts on over knitted gloves. Ready to go.

She stands on the runner tails with one hand clasping the driving bow, yanks the slipknot on the gee-line and crouches to pull the snowhook. "Okay!" Suddenly silent, the dogs dig in and pull. The end of the line whistles around the stump and they're off, a spray of snow shooting from the brake she holds down with her foot. She needs the drag on the sled to give her control going out of the yard.

The trail rises for the first couple of miles, and even the speed maniacs eventually kick back into a smooth trot. She leans over the driving bow and peers at Jeremy. His eyes are closed and his scarf is still in place, crystals of frost forming where he breathes through it. She pulls the flap tight across the top of the sled bag and presses the Velcro shut. He's sheltered from the wind, but she'll be able to hear if he starts to cry.

THE RISING SUN spins circles of light through snow-covered branches. The team curves along the trail. Katie listens to the sighing of the runners and patter of dogs' feet, and feels the crisp bite of the winter air. They're making swift progress.

She rubs the sheepskin patch on the back of her mitt against her cheeks and nose to stimulate circulation. They slope down towards the Yukon River. The team is in a groove — a steady, fast trot. There's been more snow since her last run and she squats low to skim under the weighted willows and black spruce that arch over the trail. As she goes under one, she reaches up with her mitted hand and slaps the overhang. It springs up and some of the falling snow catches under her collar and sends chills down her back.

A week ago, shivering as she hunched over the phone in the booth at the corner, Katie called home, collect. "I don't know about Christmas yet, Mom. It's hard to line somebody up to look after the dogs." It was a grey day. Wind whipped junk mail from under the tilting line of green mailboxes in the parking lot. Paper scudded south and east in a flurry of blowing snow.

"Well, if we book now we can still get an excursion fare for you." Her mother sounded so close. As Katie looked through the glass of the booth at the salvage yard across the highway, a raven sailed by on the wind. "We're dying to meet Jeremy," her mother was saying.

"I know, Mom." She pressed the phone against her ear and hugged herself.

"In the pictures you sent he looks like you did when you were a baby — except for the hair."

THE SUN ISN'T high enough to reach the stretch of trail along the river to the north of the lot, and it's much colder. They are running into the breeze now, through a patch of small pine. She wishes she hadn't been so slaphappy earlier — the back of her neck is damp and her teeth chatter when she relaxes her jaw. She pulls the wolverine-fringed hood over her musher's hat and zips up the snorkel. She sees the trail through a tunnel now, no peripheral vision, but she feels her ears and scalp start to warm.

Katie's more than halfway through her planned run, about to start the climb up from the river to the start of the second trail loop. She should decide soon if she's going to take the loop out along the Alaska Highway, or turn onto the short trail back to the tent frame.

On the uphill stretch, while the dogs slow on the grade, she bends over the driving bow to check on Jeremy. He's sleeping and his face is a healthy, rosy colour: no pale spots, no threat of frostbite. She can go on. His scarf has shifted a bit so she leans forward again to tug it up. Then she presses the Velcro tight with her left hand and straightens.

The branch hits her ruff, just above her left eye, stuns her, sweeps her off the sled and peels her hand away from the driving bow. Down on her knees she grabs at the trailing gee-line. It snakes through her mitt and leaves an undulating track in the snow. The sled and Jeremy — without her — shrink into the white funnel of trail like water down a drain.

"Whoa Copper! Whoa!" He is the only one that might stop the team. She struggles to her feet and stumbles into a run. She shouts again and again, until her voice is gone.

She throws her hood back and rips the parka open. Her face burns and salt stings her eyes. Blood pounds in her ears. Katie races to the trail junction with the second loop, praying they'll turn left and take the trail back to the lot.

There's a wide pattern of paw prints at the corner, scrapes and drag marks as if some of the dogs wanted to head for the yard. But the sled tracks swerve right, away from the trail to the tent frame. Beyond the turn, there is a continuing gouge in the trail, as if something is dragging. But there are still two runner tracks — the sled's upright.

They'll hit the highway unless she can head them off. She runs flat out towards the tent frame. She'll take the truck and head them off at the skidoo crossing.

SHE RIPS INTO the tent frame and scatters papers looking for the truck keys.

The door of the Toyota screeches open. She jams the key in the ignition, twists. It cranks, slowly, then faster. She pumps the gas. It coughs. Stumbles. Catches. She takes a deep breath — it's running — and grabs the ice scraper to clear part of the windshield.

Back in the truck, she rolls down the window and holds her breath so she won't fog the inside. She shifts into gear, feathers the clutch, and the truck moves forward. No time to get stuck. She shifts into second. The odometer whines in the cold. She has to head them off.

The truck bumps down the drive and bounces up onto the road, the back end breaking loose for a moment on the packed snow. She imagines Jeremy in the swerving sled, alone and terrified. At the highway she turns right and nails the gas pedal.

WHEN SHE GETS to the skidoo crossing Katie wheels the truck onto the shoulder and pulls tight against the snowbank. She jogs down the track to the opening in the bush. Searches the snow. There are no fresh sled tracks. Wiping her eyes and straightening, she follows the trail into the trees. "Jeremy," she croaks. She picks up her pace again.

By the time the trail angles to the east, her knees are wobbling and she has to slow to a walk. She's moving straight into the sun, blinded by the glare off the snow. She hears the dogs before she sees them and presses again into a run.

The sled is nosed into a tree, still upright, the dogs around it caught in noisy tangles. Jeremy's head gives a little start when Katie rips back the sled flap. There are salt stains under his eyes and his scarf is frosted around his mouth and nose, but he's fine. She feels her shoulders drop in relief.

When she kneels by the sled and touches her lips to his forehead he cries. "You're all right," she says as she frees him from the car seat and lifts him out. "We're okay." She hugs him, rocking gently, side to side, until he calms. Opening her parka, she tucks him tight against her, snugs up the waist drawcord and pulls up the zipper of her parka to hold him there.

Then she turns to the wailing dogs.

Copper is lying on the snow, caught behind Rickie and a couple of the large male yearlings who snap at each other and lunge against their harnesses. As they do, they pull

Copper's body back and forth. Katie realizes they've dragged him — all the way from the tent frame turn-off. Rickie pants, tongue out, small puffs of vapour rising from her muzzle. Katie frees her, then the yearlings, and finally kneels over Copper. His muzzle and tongue are crusted with snow and he lies flat and still. Katie presses her ear to the fur of his side. There's no rise, no sound. She can hardly breathe, and her tears bead on Copper's shining fur. "Thank you," she whispers as she strokes his head. The ears are stiffening.

Katie stands and turns to the other dogs. She releases snaps and sorts tangles. Some of the dogs chew at her gloved hands in panic and struggle as she loosens lines. Others quietly lick her face. Where she has to, she uses her Leatherman to cut lines and harnesses to set dogs free. They first circle, then nose away from her and trot back up the trail. Jeremy is asleep again.

Katie strips Copper's harness and then lifts him in her arms. Jeremy protests for a moment, and then accepts the pressure against his back. She pushes off the trail and into the bush, wading through the knee-deep snow to find a resting place for Copper. It's hard to carry both of them.

Back at the sled, Katie surveys the churned snow and mess of lines and harnesses. She's soaked with perspiration and trembling with fatigue. She hugs Jeremy, pulling him tight to her, and shakes her head. She shivers, and her teeth begin to chatter. "We'd better get ourselves home," she tells her son.

Before she leaves, she bundles the lines and harnesses into the sled bag. "We should be able to get something for all this," she mutters. Then she ties the sled's gee-line around her hips, leans into the load and trudges up the trail. The light is behind them and a long blue shadow points ahead, half-haloed by the sparkling snow around it. As the trail turns towards the highway, it narrows and darkens for a stretch. Then they're out of the bush and on the right-of-way, in the full brilliance of the sun. Katie can feel the warmth on her face and tilts her head back. Above them, the sky drifts like a pale blue parachute. She feels her stride lengthen as she nears the truck, and she hardly notices the pull of the sled.

The Surprising Weight of the Fall

Dean Eyre

and the forest was in the wrong
so evidently in the wrong
waving its trunks
its limbs
its branches
in the black shadowed starlight
in the shadowed snow-downed darkness
that we didn't even have to think hard about it
didn't pause between beers
pause in the deft lick and twist
of the round raspy file
as it kissed the saw's little teeth sharp
and shining
spinning like carnival stars
flicking red happy spittle
on the white
snow-downed ground

didn't have to pause
   in our steel-bloated trucks
  their bunched-up
chained-down tires
         snapping sparks from stones
         on the twisted chainsaw road
         that fell on humped and rocky hills
            fell like someone had tossed a rope
                     from a plane
            tossed a rope from 10,000 feet
     said "here's your Jesus road
            you godforsaken bastards. I hope you like it."

      and the gas can bounced
         from one end of the box
      and back again
oppressed
         ridiculous to be bounced
         from end to end
      and back again
         ridiculous to be red plastic
      to have jaunty yellow caps
absurd to be here
      in the crumpled box
      of a whining old Ford
         when in its glowing ruby hollow
         it carries the ancient liquor
         of million year old trees
         boiled down by millennia
to this fine flammable essence
         sad

to spin
    and burn
        for this

the forest was so evidently in the wrong
we had almost no choice
        but to cut
        our notches
        our counter-cut
the careful line and arc
drawn through branchless space
the push of a gloved hand
and the surprising weight of the fall

later
    by the stove
    November a frozen black hand
  pressed against
    the windowpane
lips lapped about the cool brown
        nipple of a beer
    someone with sore tired arms
says "but aint this cheerful then"
    and we all smile with our little white teeth
                and nod
    a bubble of sap explodes
    a geyser of sparks and ash
    in the dark iron heart
        of the hungry leering stove

Rented Room

Yvette Nolan

SHE'S WALKING ALONG the Warm Bay road, memorizing the view, when Horst pulls over in his big blue Cherokee.

"Angela! Angela!" he calls, pronouncing it the German way, with a hard g, the way her father had pronounced it, making her feel both childlike and fearful.

"You are going to the post office, yes? Leap in."

"Jump, Horst. Or hop."

"What?"

"Jump in. Not leap."

"Leap is wrong?"

"No, not wrong, just — it's a figure of speech, an idiom, and you have to say it a certain way. You say jump in, or hop in."

"Well, jump in, Angela."

Angela slides into the Jeep.

"Thank you, Angela. I worry I will never learn to think in English."

"Idioms are hard."

"Idioms are idiots."

Angela considers correcting him — *idiotic* — but laughs instead. It's a game they play whenever they run into each other at community events, when they find themselves together, the two outsiders participating but not quite part of, more audience than actors in the social life of Atlin. Although he must be fifty, nearly twice her age, Angela plays the role of teacher, and Horst the good student. Angela never corrects him twice on the same grammatical or syntactical error.

Angela snaps her seat belt home and the Jeep kicks up a great spray of crush behind them.

"You were dreaming."

"Sort of," Angela smiles. "I was memorizing."

"Memorizing?"

"Yes, I was memorizing Atlin, because I have to go."

"Go? Away from Atlin? Where?"

"I don't know, Horst. But winter is coming on and I can't camp outside much longer. So I have to go."

"But where will you go? You have a job somewhere?"

"No. No job. I suppose I'll look for waitressing work somewhere for the winter."

"You can not longer work at the Cedar Rest?"

"No longer," Angela says, watching a tornado of leaves spin across the road and into the ditch. "It's been really slow since the season ended. Roger had to let me go."

THE CEDAR REST has been a pretty good job, for Atlin. It's the only restaurant in town, part of the gravel strip

mall that houses the Cedar Rest gas pumps, the Cedar Rest
Garage, and the Cedar Rest Laundry and Showers. Angela
had stumbled into the Rest one hot May day looking for a
bathroom, having just inhaled 100 kilometres of dust on the
back of a motorcycle belonging to a guy who'd heard there
was *this back-to-the-land artsy-fartsy community* tucked
away just off the Alaska Highway. She hadn't planned the
detour, she was actually headed to Whitehorse, or maybe
Dawson City, but the biker she hooked up with at Liard
Hotsprings had said he just wanted to drive through, and
the guidebook in Angela's pack referred to Atlin as "The
Switzerland of the North," so she figured it was worth a look.

On her way back to the biker, she helped a German
tourist translate her incomprehensible menu into a meal,
and the proprietor, short-handed and desperate, offered
her a job on the spot. Always open to the signs, and rapidly
tiring of the biker's *whatever* attitude, Angela took the job,
figuring she'd stay a few weeks, pocket a little money, and
then continue north.

Over the summer, Angela discovered that the tourist
trade is mostly German. Not that there is ever much tourist
trade; even at the height of high season, the tourists are
limited to those few happy campers who fancy themselves
adventurers and are not daunted by the damage that an hour
on the dead-end crush road that leads to Atlin can do to
their RVs.

By mid-August, the steady trickle had all but dried up.
Now, just shy of Labour Day, Angela is without visible, or
invisible, means of support.

HORST PULLS UP in front of the post office. As usual, there's a gathering around the door, and Angela sees several of the women turn and mark her presence in Horst's car. But she also sees Linda in the flock and she feels a pleasant flutter of anticipation. Linda is the local den-mother, and she ushered Angela into Atlin society, inviting her up to her place at Lina Creek, stopping by the campsite with vegetables from her garden, insisting Angela accompany her to community events. Angela opens her door and looks back at Horst.

"Horst? You coming in?"

"Ja. In a minute. I am thinking."

"Okay."

"Angela!" Linda cries as she walks up the path to the post office, "I thought of you this morning when I saw the frost. I thought, I hope Angela's sleeping bag is rated for winter camping."

"Hey Angela," Bob says as he pushes through the screen door, "bet it was pretty fresh up there this morning."

"It was fresh, all right," she says, nodding to Bob who drops the door shut behind him.

"You know, I've got another sleeping bag you can have," Linda says. "I don't think the cold is here to stay, we've probably got another month of summer."

Fifteen minutes later, Linda looks at her watch.

"Oops, look at the time. I promised Miss Lori I'd come by before lunch. D'you want a lift somewhere?"

Angela shakes her head.

"Well, come by Lina Creek tomorrow," Linda says. "You can help me can, and I'll dig up another sleeping bag."

"Okay," Angela says, but Linda is already down the stairs. Angela turns her face to the August sun and closes her eyes. She considers opening one of her mother's letters, but even the thought of having to hear her mother's hurt and bewildered tone in her head exhausts her and instead she tucks the two violet envelopes into her jacket pocket and looks up to see Horst sitting in the Cherokee, still as stone.

"Horst?" she taps on his window. "You okay?"

"Angela," he says. "Come to my house for lunch. I will make you sausages and eggs, ja? and we will talk."

"Lunch?"

"Ja, jump in."

Suddenly, Angela is ravenous. When she lost her job at the Rest, she also lost her daily hot meal. She's been hoarding her meagre summer earnings for whatever her next step is, a bus ticket to Edmonton or a month's rent in Whitehorse, so she's really been living on pasta and rice. She's been up to Linda's, twice, but Linda's been so good to her, she's trying to not wear out her welcome. Trying not to look desperate. She realizes her mouth is watering. She slides into the Jeep again.

ANGELA HAS NEVER been to Horst's house, although she knows which one it is because the locals love to crow over the amenities it has — four-piece bathroom that requires water to be trucked in, an island in the kitchen, and one wall that is a huge stone fireplace, *big enough to roast a whole sheep in,* the locals have confided to her, although now that she sees it, she reckons it would have to be a pretty small sheep — and over the fact that a foreigner, a German, has bought such prime land in Atlin. From the outside, it is impressive enough, a round house crafted of round logs, high above the ground on round posts. Inside, it is breathtaking, and surprisingly unlike what Angela thought Horst to be. Horst seems so practical, so efficient, yet his house is fanciful and romantic. It is warm and amber-coloured, with high ceilings that give it a faintly cathedral-like feel. In addition to the grand picture window that frames a stunning view of Atlin Lake and the usual assortment of pedestrian kitchen and bathroom casements, the house boasts eight smaller windows all the way around the circumference of the house. The late summer sun pours in through the little portholes.

"Oh wow," she says.

"Yes," Horst says. "It is the best time of year for the little windows. The sun is just right in the sky; the light seems to come in sideways."

"It's beautiful, Horst."

"The architect thought it was a waste. Unnecessary. But he never was here this time of year. "

Horst busies himself in the kitchen, pulling food out of the fridge and stacking it on the island behind him.

"It is my favourite time of year in Atlin."

"Is it?" Angela says. "I imagine spring is lovely, too."

"Except for spring."

"And the summer was amazing."

"Yes, I like summer too."

Angela laughs. "Is there a season you don't like in Atlin, Horst?"

"I don't like winter, because I cannot stay in Atlin."

"Like me," Angela says.

Horst busies himself over the gas stove, meticulously lining up sausages in a pan, slicing thick slabs of fresh white bread, melting butter in another pan and arranging four brown eggs beside it.

"You are Cherman, Angela?"

"My father is from Germany, yes. He left after the war."

"After the war."

"Yes."

"And your mother?"

"German descent."

"So you are Cherman."

"Well, I think of myself as Canadian."

Finally, *finally,* he puts the plate of sausages and eggs down in front of her.

"Thanks, Horst."

Angela cuts the meat in bits with the side of her fork, shovels great mouthfuls of hot food into her mouth.

"Aren't you eating?" she asks, around a mouthful of egg and bread and meat.

"No, no," Horst says, lifting the last two sausages onto her plate. "Coffee? Or tea?"

"Tea. No, coffee, if it's the real stuff. I can't make a decent cup of coffee in the campground."

Horst turns and begins to spoon espresso into a small maker.

"There are two more eggs on the stove."

"No, thanks," she says, but reaches for another piece of bread to mop up her plate.

Horst turns the gas on under the coffee pot, and without looking at Angela, says, "I have a pro-po-si-tion for you."

"Okay," Angela says.

"I am Cherman. You are Cherman."

Angela shrugs.

"I live here half the year, in Chermany I do business the other half."

Angela waits.

"You do not want to leave Atlin, but you must, because you must find work."

Is this a job offer? Angela wonders. Does he want me to go to Germany with him?

"I have no child, Angela, I am 53 years old. I have not the time to find a wife, to keep a wife. To do the things necessary to keep a wife happy. But I have very much to offer to a child. And I want to leave my business, my houses, to my child."

He pauses for an instant, but it is a short, businesslike pause, very much a pause her father would take in the midst of a dissertation. Horst reminds her very much of her father, Angela decides.

"Here is my proposition. You will stay here, in my house, over this winter. You will have my baby. I will pay you $30,000 to have my baby."

Angela stops chewing the bread in her mouth, looks at Horst. Suddenly, she is acutely aware of her body, of a piece of gristle from the sausage stuck between her molars, of the gluey yolk on her fingers that still hold a piece of bread now sodden with grease, of the lump of heavy food in her stomach. She feels her stomach begin to do a slow forward roll, feels nausea pluck at her gorge, and then she laughs. Horst laughs too.

"You're kidding, right?"

"No," he says, smiling and nodding, "no, I am not kidding. I will pay you $30,000 to stay in my house and have my baby. I know a doctor who will come and do the fertilization."

Angela gets up off the stool at the island, pushes the plate away, grabs her jacket. The two violet envelopes pop out of her pocket and slide across the kitchen floor to Horst's feet. He bends to pick them up.

"I gotta go," she says. From one knee, Horst proffers the envelopes. She takes them and stuffs them back in her pocket. "Thanks for lunch."

WALKING BACK UP the Warm Bay road, Angela counts the steps to the Pine Creek bridge. And then stops. As a child, she counted incessantly — steps to school, dog poos on the boulevard, number of times her father said no in an evening — and falling back into her counting habit is childish. She continues her walk, naming the colours and variations of colours in the leaves along the side of the road and up Monarch Mountain: red yellow orange gold goldenrod copper sienna scarlet … and then stops, realizing that she's enumerating the colours of her childhood Crayola Crayons. "Oh grow up," she whispers. She waves at Linda as she passes her on the road, and then waves her on when she sees her brake lights flashing scarlet … scarlet, there she goes again with the Crayolas.

In the campground, she sits at the wooden picnic table next to her two-person tent. She resists the impulse to tidy up the campsite that is festooned with the detritus of her life: frypan leaning against the rocks of the firepit, sleeping bag airing out on the table, her Cedar Rest uniform, as clean as it will ever get, drying on a jerry-rigged clothesline strung between two pine trees. Her mother would be mortified if she could see how she lived.

Her mother is mortified, without the benefit of having seen her campsite at the Pine Creek Campground.

ANGELA IS AN only child, a late child, who arrived three days short of her mother's forty-third birthday. Long resigned to childlessness, her parents saw her as a miracle, and treated her accordingly, cherishing her and overprotecting her. Her father, ten years her mother's senior, poured the aspirations and expectations of a new Canadian into his daughter. Blessed with absolute faith in the unlimited possibility of Canada, he was disappointed in Angela's failure to apply herself, by her lack of desire to *become* something. She dawdled through a couple of liberal arts degrees, first at a prairie university in her home town and then a west-coast university, but at the age of twenty-seven she was still without the accessories that would signal Canadian success to her parents: a career, a house, a husband, and children.

NOW SHE SITS, tapping her mother's violet envelopes against the burnt umber picnic table. Finally, she opens them to ascertain which one was written first, and then reads them in the wrong order. As she finishes each lotion-scented page, she drops it beside her and they dance away in the breeze. Then she sits, still, so still that Peggy driving up the road will later tell Linda that she gave her quite a start because she was looking right at her for ages before she realized it was a person sitting there. Angela sees Peggy's brake lights, sees her throw the car into reverse and start to back up. It is all she can do to raise her hand and wave Peggy on. I'm fine, she thinks, forcing a smile, an attitude of well-being, so that Peggy will *just drive on, drive on.* This is me, fine, just sitting here enjoying the failing light, the falling leaves, the promise of dew on the air. Peggy stops, then raises her hand and drives off.

Finally, Angela extricates herself from the wooden table and digs a thick sweater out of her knapsack. She decides to build a fire, and walks to the entranceway of the campground where they store the wood, and then keeps walking down the Warm Bay Road.

THE FIRST STARS are winking themselves into existence when Angela comes into view of Horst's house, the high portholes like amber beacons in the night, shining in every direction. It's cooling off fast, and she can see her breath as she walks up the driveway. Linda told her there'd be northern lights soon, so she scans the heavens. She stands on the doorstep and raises her hand to knock, but lays it instead on the sturdy wooden door. From inside she can hear classical music, could be Bach cello, imagines she can feel the bass notes humming through the door and into her palm. She knocks and there is the sound of Horst, his voice moving from the kitchen to the doorway.

"Hallo? Come in. Come in."

But she doesn't come in and finally the door opens and the butterlight spills out and pours over Angela, washing out the stars and the night sky.

Final Move

Tory Russell

LONG TERM CARE is terminal care. I'm working here at
your new home when you move in.

You arrive with life crowded around you. It has carved
deep; it is a well-worn trail, up and down your spine. It
follows secret passages through your caved chest, under
slumped shoulders. It still demands of you and you of it.
Although you can no longer live alone, still, sometimes
effortlessly, you do astonishing things: you nimbly climb
into a van, you do a set of eight steps, take a leak in the
bush. Down at the water's edge you clean a fish, your hands
moving from ancient memory. Blood spills on your white
shoe. I hand you the knife, the towel. Sometimes you see so
well. A bird, nesting across the way ... a memory surfaces
clear and colourful. You tell a story.

Here at the end of your life, your character carved and
true, here where it is too late, it almost doesn't matter to

me who you were, I cannot pass judgement. We meet where worlds connect. This is a staging area: you are leaving, and I am the midwife of your leave-taking. I translate to you the institution, the schedule, the hum, the bells.

We go for a ride in the car. Nice, quiet, open road. Near your home, you tell me where to go, which doors to knock on. I look back and your face is small in the car window. Sitting low in the seat, your face hovers, disembodied, over the sill.

No answer. We drive on. You remember all this country, your hand gestures a slow, small motion, with thin, stretched fingers that don't bend easily. You have walked over all this land, in all moods and weathers. You have slept on it. I ask questions about the area, for it is new to me. But your answers are vague, the trails you know do not tie in with the new road that I know. You know the contours, the gullies where water runs, you remember it before the forest.

We swing by your old place.

"How long did you live here?" I ask.

"Forever."

The place is set up but vacant, with a thin dust. Your hand flits lightly over shelves, through drawers. It's like you just stepped out for a moment.

"Let's bring these pictures back," I say.

"No."

"Heeeyy — how 'bout this cowboy hat?"

"No."

I peer at old photos. I want to ask about the pretty women fading. But I don't. I don't ask for any more detail than you offer.

I wish I could bring this view back to your room in Long Term Care. These mountains of yours could watch over you better than the apartments across the way. Your new room has no pictures on the wall, no memories, only the calendar it came with.

You are what you have always been. You are the same bones and teeth, eye sockets and valves, the same nervous system patterns learned and repeated. You are still all of this.

Over time, I get to know your moods; they cross you like weather over the land. Short confessions and quick tears pass before I'm even sure they're there. Tea, Kleenex, tools of this trade. A lifetime of wisdom, of lessons learned, might not help you now.

In the smoke room you tell one of the staff, "I'm gonna die soon." She consoles you, "No you're not, only the good die young." I see you smile then, and I am thrilled.

Here at the end of life, you can still be the butt of a joke, you still hope for a certain meal, you watch others and ask about them, or you just stare quietly from a window out on the road. We all do it, now and again.

In here, everyone has a case history, a chart. There are questionnaires, assessments, care plans…. "Self-inflicted," your condition is marked. But when you said to me,

"Country music's all I understand," you told me more than the file ever could.

In the car we go to funerals, old friends passing. You come alive in other people then. They see you, and it all comes back to them. They come up close, they crowd you, they ask, "Where ya been, ya still like vodka?" breathing in your face.

"Remember when I was a teenager? Remember what you showed me?"

"Aaaaugh I remember you." One of them is shaking your hand over and over; you are so precious to him. You are his own memories intact.

"Is that your girlfriend?" Teasing.

They look at me, eyes shining, faces smiling to share, but I cannot. I am only happy to see that they are happy to see you. Other folks are suspicious, and they are right. There is so much I do not know, and worse, there are some things I might know. Some people see only who you used to be, and cannot conceal their dismay. To me, you are long past what the rest of us cannot live without, long past approval.

Back at the place, we sit, smoke and drink tea. I know that you do not know my name, but you accept me, we are somehow companions. I know some of the signs on the road you travel. I watch for your stumble, for when you lose your words, when you repeat more, remember less. I watch for when you need my hand, a wheelchair, help with your spoon. I monitor the impatience, the resignation, the light in your eyes.

You are leaving. I give you my hand so that you can let go.

Exit Slowly, Pursued By Bears

Jerome Stueart

WHEN MICHAEL COMES into his darkened house to phone his girlfriend, he doesn't see his wife Anne sitting at the kitchen table watching him. She freezes, pulling in all her agitation until she is another piece of unmoveable furniture in this house. She pinches a snowy owl feather between her fingers, the final piece of her daughter's Hallowe'en costume she'd come back to retrieve.

He has no clue she's in the room.

Out the window, she can see his partner, Hugh, sitting in the squad car. Michael rolls shotgun shells in his palm, snapping them together. She can't see him clearly because the power is off again from the wind blowing the power lines around. He's using his cell phone, she thinks, so he won't be detected except by the phone bill which she never reads. In the shadows, she hears him walk to the gun case and choose a shotgun, hears the squeak of the glass door. He laughs into the phone, a confident laugh that Anne hasn't heard for seven years—not since they were dating, really.

"You know you are," Michael says to the woman. "Very bad."

He's whispering, but Anne bets he doesn't know why. Everyone can feel a body in the room with them, even in the dark. Bodies give off a presence, a wall of sorts, and you pick it up like a bat bouncing sonar.

"I'll see you tonight," he says to her. She's a fellow RCMP. Well, that makes sense, Anne thinks.

When the spotlight from Michael's squad car flips on and blasts through the uncurtained double-paned window, Anne knows it is the hand of God coming to reveal her silent, prying, accidental body in the chair at the kitchen table. She braces herself. She already feels guilty just hearing this conversation, but now she's going to be forced to confront him with it, right here, in the dining room. The light passes over the framed pictures on the wall, one by one, swinging and swooping to the right till it falls off the dining room wall and slaps her in the face, covering her body in white. After lingering on her, the light bounces to the refrigerator and disappears, like the hand of God should disappear. Michael sees nothing. His back is turned at the critical moment when she is revealed.

Hugh honks the horn, and Michael tells the woman he loves her and hangs up. He walks through the house, not even brushing the furniture with his heavy down coat, shuts the door behind him, joins his partner in a quick repartee and two car doors slam. Two beams, lesser hands of God, brush her shoulders and turn out into the cold snow.

Anne waits a few minutes. Just as she expected, the lights come back on as if on cue. She puts on her coat. The lights glare. She looks around the room, at everything they own, and feels another presence there, as if someone else has been in that chair, or on that sofa, or left infrared footprints across the carpet. Anne snatches the feather and runs out of the house, slamming the door, locking every bolt. She stands at the door and wonders who she is locking out.

IN A FEW moments the woman on the phone, the rookie police officer newly assigned to Arrow Downs, Manitoba, will be playing a wendigo in the haunted house and scaring twenty-five children in a typecast role, Anne thinks. The bright colours of the community centre do nothing to cheer her as she comes in and takes off her coat. She misses the hook, and her coat falls stiffly on the galoshes of adult workers.

Anne is in charge this year, in charge of all the bobbing, the pinning of tails, the balloon busting, beanbag tossing, baseball pitching, all the sick children after they devour cookies and brownies and miniature "bite-size" candies. Why they have to go door-to-door later for the same food, Anne doesn't know.

Part of her job this year is to organize the volunteers. She gives them direction. Her presence is supposed to provide some form of order. She walks down the aisles between children darting and bobbing. There's a fortune teller set up in the corner. Anne imagines her telling girls who their cheating husbands will be, when they will cheat on them, for how long, and how much of a divorce settlement they'll get.

She doesn't even see the blur of activity around her as she escapes into the centre's expansive kitchen and collapses into a chair.

Her daughter, Rachel, in her Pocahontas outfit, sees her and runs into the kitchen asking about her feather. Her mother hands over the feather and Rachel dances back into the festivities of shouts and splashes of apple water, explosions of balloons. In five minutes they will gather all the children together for the haunted house, and the carnival-booth volunteers will tidy up here and run home to prepare their houses for the children's arrival. It's too much for Anne tonight; she would much rather she and Rachel could decline and just go to bed.

Anne pushes herself out of the kitchen with a cup of coffee in one hand. With a practised smile, she rings the bell for "Haunted House" and the collection of twenty-five children runs into the hallway, dropping everything to be first. There are fifteen volunteers in the haunted house who are dressed up like ghouls. And Caroline, one marriage-wrecking witch, Anne thinks, moving around in the dark, trying to make the children have little "bite-size" heart attacks in their brightly coloured costumes. Just enough scares to make the children very happy.

The entrance to the haunted house is a long tunnel where kids have to crawl through on hands and knees. Black garbage bags hang beside the tunnel, blocking off the normally large hallway. Anne lets the children in by fives, shooting them like pinballs into the game. Her daughter backs out of the tube, deftly crawling over three children in the tunnel's entrance.

"A witch with teeth and long hands — she tried to take me away," Rachel says when she's out, her feather bent backward by the tunnel roof.

"She's just playing," Anne tells her. Her daughter is beginning to cry, not at all the brave Pocahontas she pretends to be tonight. Her brown hair comes out of her braids, clinging to her face. Anne picks her up. "She won't eat you," Anne tells her.

"She won't eat us?"

"No," Anne says like a mantra she's repeating for herself. "She won't eat us. She won't eat us."

Anne doesn't feel like crawling in to see Caroline on her hands and knees. They walk through the adult workers' entrance into the complete chaos of the haunted house. Children are being chased from three consecutive rooms: Dracula's Crypt, The Swamp Monster's Lair and the Mad Doctor's Surgery Room. Lava lamps light Dracula's Crypt, the walls shimmer flourescently through the smoke of dry ice in The Swamp Monster's Lair, and a strobe light breaks the Mad Doctor's chase scene into still frames. Kids, little devils and heroes and angels and Barbie dolls, are running mad, trying to find the exit, shooting out of the tunnel into the haunted house and bouncing between the vampire and the deep green swamp. Anne crosses through the madness with powerful strides, with more speed and determination than she's been able to muster in weeks. She's heading for the wendigo that meets the kids at the tunnel's exit. She's going to pull off the mask and reveal something for Rachel and something for herself. You're scaring us, she's going to say. You're scaring us to death.

"Caroline," she yells over the din and motions the figure in the light-splotched darkness over to the side. The figure stands; Anne sees a giant pig's head mounted on a broom handle, stuck through the back of someone's shirt, walking towards her. The figure has long fake spindly arms. This is not what she expects. Even she is frightened.

"Who are you?" she asks, fully expecting something supernatural to happen.

A head pops out of the shirt and it is Scott Jasper, whose parents own the café downtown. His hair is matted on his head.

"Yeah, how goes the battle?" he asks.

"Where's Caroline? I thought she was supposed to be a wendigo. And what are you?"

He beams. "I'm the Lord of the Flies, can't you tell?"

The pig's head scowls and she swears she sees it bleeding at the bottom. She knows because of the smell that it is a real pig's head. "What are you doing bringing that in here?"

"I want to be authentic — "

"This is a haunted house. If we wanted authenticity, we would have held this in a cemetery. Get that out of here. It stinks," she says, but Rachel, scared Rachel, is reaching up to pet the head on the stick.

"No," Anne pulls her away. "Don't touch it." She turns to him. "That's fresh, isn't it?"

Scott looks up at the pig's head. An expression of appreciation and admiration crawls across his face. "You noticed! We brought it back from my uncle's farm this summer — a whole pig. I froze the head, and thawed it out for tonight. Wanted it as fresh as it could be. Nothing less for the kids," he adds, putting his hands on his hips. "Well, if that's all, I'll go back to my job."

She grabs his arm. "You should go over to the high school and bother your friends." She doesn't want to march this thing to the room's exit. When Scott turns his back, the whole body looks freakishly real, the head slightly out of synch with the body, so that the pig watches her even as Scott has turned away.

She finds the energy to push him out the door into another hallway.

"Caroline couldn't make it. She asked me," he says, his feelings obviously hurt.

"Where is she?" Anne asks quickly, pulling Rachel close.

"They needed all the cops and the conservation officers tonight," he says, "for the trick-or-treat." But she only half hears him. What she thinks is this: Caroline and Michael are together.

Anne doesn't know what to say, and shuts the door on Scott standing alone in the hallway, the head nodding a second opinion as she leaves. Rachel hides her face on Anne's shoulder. As if that protected anyone, Anne thinks, and they fumble through the black garbage bags and back into the light.

The carnival workers pack up supplies and trash, and wrap themselves in coats to prepare their homes for the surprise of trick-or-treaters.

RACHEL, THE BRAVE Little Pocahontas, doesn't want to trick-or-treat now. She's afraid of the bears outside, spotlights or not, police officers with loaded rifles or not, groups of people or not. Pocahontas knows a bad deal going down.

"Can she ride with you?" Anne asks Michael outside the community centre. He radioes the officer who will drive the streets alongside the trick-or-treaters, in the north part of town.

"She doesn't want to trick-or-treat?" he asks, looking at the little girl in the huge pink coat. "You don't want to trick-or-treat?"

"There are bears," Rachel says.

"Bears. See?" Anne holds out her hand to her husband as if this is what will convince him. "She's petrified. Can she stay with you? I have to go." She doesn't wait for an answer, but turns and runs towards four huddled children in their bright winter coats.

"Yeah," he says to his daughter after Anne leaves. "Can you take the back and watch through the window for me?" He opens the car door slowly, and Rachel jumps in the back seat, skittling to the middle. The car is warm. A round spotlight mounted on the roof hangs over the passenger door, blinking like an eye when Michael passes his hand over the lens.

They've divided the kids into six groups, four children apiece, a manageable size for a chaperone, and not too overwhelming for the homeowner in charge of dropping candy in their bags. They have amassed the three RCMP in town and two conservation officers to watch the kids as they go trick-or-treating. With polar bears frequenting the town on their way to Hudson Bay, the police wanted to protect the children. So, they will come along, escorts to the trick-or-treating, as if every child is a visiting dignitary.

"Ready, Group One?" Michael radioes the mother in charge of Group One. The spotlights shoot down the dark spaces in between the houses to catch any wandering bear that might be lurking. "Group One is ready," radioes Mrs. Patton.

Anne looks on from a distance. Group One, as if being filmed in a scene for a movie, comes on stage through Spotlight One and goes up to the door of the Brenners' house. Snow flickers in the yellow porchlight. Enter Mrs. Brenner, all smiles, bowl of candy in one hand, coat and muffler around her throat. No one thinks to say, "We just saw you, not twenty minutes ago, with the darts and balloons." Instead they yell a raucous "Trick or Treat!" Children giggle appropriately, thrusting their bags open, and the devil sneezes twice. Snickers and Milky Ways leap into bags. It's a great shot. They file away after Mrs. Brenner smiles and waves, moving through a beam of light dotted with snow and disappearing into darkness. Car Two picks them up at House Two, spotlights and all, and the whole scene is repeated with the Petersens, who add some pizzazz to the kids' entry by shouting with delight.

It's as if the whole world is faking just as much as Anne. She looks over at Michael — far, far away from her. A whole house is between them. He diminishes in the shadows behind the spotlight. Even his arm has disappeared behind the car.

The squad cars and conservation trucks line up as if they are invading these homes. Anne shivers in her down coat.

Michael turns to Rachel in the back of the squad car.

"You sure you don't want to do this? There's no bears out, you know." She looks out the window and watches the children foosh through snow in the front yards of houses ripe with surprise. And she sees the spotlights bordering each yard like walls, and she sees the officer's rifle in his left hand.

"I'm okay," she says.

In Arrow Downs, Manitoba it takes a map to get the kids to every family participating in the trick-or-treat. Anne has designed a route that winds around the town and spirals towards the centre. Circular paths are always better for kids than straight ones. Circles make things last longer. She has given a copy of this map to the five officers who will be following them. She laughs when she thinks about it: there are more officers in Arrow Downs than there are firemen. More officers than clergymen. She watches Michael get into the car. Anne can see the feather on top of Rachel's head quiver back and forth.

IT IS LATER in the evening, with fourteen houses done. It's a good thing they give the kids black garbage bags to collect their loot. Anything less would have to be emptied and recycled again and again. Michael sets up his car at the next set of houses. After each officer is through with a house, they move to the top of the line, five houses further along the route, sometimes on the next street. They're trying to cover all the bases. Caroline pulls up beside him in a few moments, no one in her back seat. Michael rolls his windows up to seal the car and steps out to set up the lights.

"Why do you have Rachel?" Caroline asks him, peering into the back of the car.

"She's afraid."

"Of your wife?" Caroline jokes and Michael laughs. She has a loud laugh that he loves to hear; it echoes, though, off the homes around them like a siren. Bold, vivacious, she has a spark that he never knew a woman could have. Anne seemed to go into mother mode as soon as they had Rachel. Not that he'd experienced neglect as a husband, but the focus was all off. The spotlight was on their child, never their marriage. And Anne, she disappeared somewhere in the shadows of motherhood. He didn't understand why — why they couldn't still be MichaelAnne as they had been to their friends. Or how drudgery could just cover their lives so quickly, turning everything bad, like brown spots on bananas.

"I'm glad you could join us," he tells her. "We were going to be short a car and I hate to do this with only four cars. It doesn't give us a lot of response time." Five cars allow one to be busy with children, one to be moving, one to be setting up and two cars to act as scouts for the whole area. Often, they have their spotlights on and flash them around, hoping that they reflect off a bear between the bushes or behind the swingsets. They want to catch him before he surprises them all.

She turns on her spotlight in the next driveway. "I was supposed to be eating babies in the haunted house. God, what happened to just plain old witches? Aren't they good enough anymore? Don't they rate? You have to have a cannibal in your haunted house," she says.

"Anne's brilliance again," he said. "It's a northern thing. Coming from the States you probably haven't heard much about wendigos."

"Thank you, no. I'll just have my little gingerbread house and Hansel and Gretel; at least the witch in that story didn't get the kids." She looks back at Rachel, who blinks at her and rubs her nose. "I really don't like her here," she sighs, then quickly corrects herself. "I mean — I like her. She's cute and kid-like and everything. But I would really like to lay one on you right now."

He looks over his shoulder to look for the other cars, but can't see beyond the bend in the road. They are safe. He glances back at Caroline and tips the spotlight directly into his own car, washing Rachel in white, and then flips it all the way around. He hopes she doesn't see the kiss.

She rolls down the window. "I'm blind."

"Close the window," he says.

"I see spots," she says, rubbing her eyes. "Daddy, um, can I have some candy?"

"Roll the window back up. It's cold out here. I don't have any candy for you, Raitch."

"I see spots, big blue and white spots," she says. He regrets flashing her now. He wishes she had a colouring book.

"The spots are moving behind the house," she says.

Caroline has reached into her car to get a gun. He turns to see them. Like ghosts, two polar bear flanks emerge in the alley behind the house, pass a fence post, and disappear.

"I saw that," he says.

Anne has radioed ahead to Michael that there is a hold-up at the Becketts' house. Tommy Kaglulak's bag broke and for three houses he's been trailing candies. It wasn't a huge break, more like a slow leak. They're trying to find all the pieces. When polar bears are on their way to Hudson Bay, they are starving. Soon the ice will freeze on the bay and they can go prowling around for seals. Until then, they are trapped inland. Anne has seen them at the dump, or in town, appearing between trailers, nosing a parked car, even running behind a car at a healthy pace. Polar bears have amazing noses. They can smell a seal from miles away. They will find Snickers buried in the snow. They will follow children who smell like food.

But Anne can't raise Michael or Caroline on the radio.

"Damn," she whispers, blowing steam across her face. She didn't think it could happen tonight. Sure, it probably happened already. He's slept with her. But on Hallowe'en? When they are busy? Why now?

And where is Rachel for all this? Anne can't help imagining her daughter, asleep in the car, abandoned by Michael. She's in a car all by herself, getting gradually colder and colder.

Anne sits in the car for a few minutes, then hangs up the radio and walks into the chaos around her. Is everything a haunted house?

Children and officers are kneeling down, looking for candy. Officers shine spotlights into each area before they allow children to look. It also helps reveal the candy, dark against the snow. They are pitching candy into a new bag that Tommy holds open as he walks from person to person

collecting chocolate bars and caramels. The children call
out as they find a piece, some as far away as two houses
down. They kneel among the bird baths pawing the ground
around their own minute-old footprints. Except for Tommy,
Anne is the only one standing and no one asks her to help.
Hucks does ask her to step to the side, he's found a flattened
Almond Joy under her boot. Anne watches everything
carefully, but sees nothing. The children are pink and purple
and blue blurs in the snow. The officers are black blurs
bobbing up and down. Tommy becomes so fast he's invisible.

IN HIS CALMEST voice, Michael says, "Hey, Rachel, why
don't you stay here? Caroline and me, we'll go and check out
a couple of houses down that way. You okay in there?"

Rachel is tired and has stretched out on the back seat.
She nods.

Michael opens the door, then shuts it tight again and
locks her in the car. The doors won't open from the back.
Hermetic, he thinks. She rolls over, wrapping her coat
around her. He'll just be gone a few minutes, so he leaves the
car running. Exhaust drifts from the tailpipe like a feather,
crooking at the end because of the cold.

Michael radioes the officers currently with the trick-or-
treaters from Caroline's car.

"I have two bears, at least, on Spring Street, going north
in the alley. Could Hugh circle around to Tay Street and see
if they've gone over there?"

Gus Davis, a veteran bear hunter, answers back, "We're
going to send the kids inside homes and join you."

"I knew you'd want to play, Gus," he says, signing off and shutting the doors of the car.

He joins Caroline four houses down. She hasn't seen the bears again, and she's worried they have stopped along the way.

"We should go into the alley behind the houses," she recommends. They both carry tranquilizer rifles, and a real gun on their belts. Sometimes a bear won't stop just because you shoot it with tranquilizers.

"I've got Hugh circling around on Tay." They decide to walk up the Donaldsons' wide driveway, leading around to the back. They walk as if the land is brittle beneath their feet, and the snow crunches with every step. They can see the whole backyard to the fence, and they shine flashlights all around.

Something shakes the ground with a steady beat. The Jaspers' house on the other side of the alley is pulsating with bright yellow light. Like a lit stage, the glass door of the balcony reveals a party of teenagers. A girl with pink hair and a blue tanktop passes something to two boys slumped on a couch. The whole thing becomes surreal when a giant pig's head comes into view in the room, looming over the couch. Scott Jasper puffs on something, and the smoke acts like a scarf, strangling the pig's head.

The girl, noticing Scott, obviously asks him to stop dripping blood on the carpet. She stands, points to the glass door, and probably yells, and Michael doesn't need to hear the sound to understand her anger. He's seen Anne a thousand days like this. The door slides open and the music rushes out into a silent neighbourhood. The thumping bass of a rap song reverberates off every house. That should scare anything roaming around, Michael thinks.

"Hey, officers. Why the guns? Are you invading?" Scott asks them from the balcony, waving. He's obviously high. He makes no attempt to hide the marijuana.

Michael and Caroline walk to the back fence of the neighbour's house, looking around carefully.

"Scott, were you just outside a few minutes ago?" Michael calls from below.

"Anne kicked me out of the haunted house, Mike. I would have gone to the high school but they're a bunch of losers." He takes a drag off the joint. "You wanna come up? I won't tell if you won't tell."

Caroline has found a set of bear prints in the alley. There's no fence around Scott's house and the bear prints lead toward the house.

"Scott, did you see any bears while you were out?"

"I'm a bear." He holds out his arms and the long spindly attachments stretch out around him. "We're all bears tonight."

Caroline comes running from the other side of the house and Michael can tell she's upset.

"Get them all out on the balcony," she yells. "All out. On the balcony. Everyone."

Scott leans the pig's head over the railing to give her their best scowl, his and the pig's above him. "What are you yelling about down there? Why are you so excited? You just want to wreck a good house," he pauses, then adds, "party. God, you're all like judges."

The other teenagers have walked out onto the balcony to see what's happening, who Scott is talking to. They surround him like a posse.

"You're all judges." He turns to his friends. "They're judges. Well, I judge you. I am the Lord of the Bears." One four-and-a-half foot arm with a claw at the end extends down toward Michael and Caroline, who are now in the yard.

Caroline says, "Michael, they're following Scott. He left the door open. They're in the house."

TWO YEARS AGO the officers postponed festivities while they relocated a wandering bear, so tonight, all of them expected the possibility. Kids and parents calmly comply with the officers' requests and merge with the warmth of the nearest house to rest and wait for the call that says the officers are done, the bears are gone, the streets are safe from scary things.

Anne, however, rebels. She cannot sit in Mrs. Gilly's house, talk about embroidery, and supervise eight children while her daughter is alone in a car and her husband is with Caroline. She is sure that Rachel has been forgotten. She pretends a run to the washroom and instead goes out the deck exit from the master bedroom. She walks down the deck stairs, out of the yard and towards the Donaldsons' house. No moonshine, but the snow is lighter than the sky. The wind has picked up considerably, blowing colder and louder than before. She walks quickly, telling herself what she will say when she sees him.

Why did you leave her alone? The question she could
have asked herself. Why did she put Rachel in Michael's car?
Bears happen. All the time. One minute you are throwing
snowballs, the next minute you are running for your life.
The street lamps arch like the antennae of each house. She
looks around for bears, for danger in this calm row of squat
multicoloured homes. Something could come out of a door.
Just like a person. In every house she saw the potential for
a door opening and a bear emerging, the house abandoned
and ransacked.

MICHAEL CALLS UP to the teenagers on the balcony. "Shut
the glass door. Shut the door. The glass door."

They laugh.

Scott waggles a claw at him, a claw made of paper and
wire. "What did we do this time? You have to learn to be
more lenient, more laid back with people and their mistakes,
Mike. No one's robbing a house, no one's — "

"Shut up," the girl tells him, slapping him on the arm. "I
wanna hear what they have to say."

"There are bears in your house and you need to shut the
glass — "

"God, that's a good one. I like that," one boy says to the
others.

The other boy is quicker. He leaps to the door and shuts
it quickly, saving them all from a bloody conclusion to this
slow, plotless horror movie. The bear sticks his nose into
their party snacks.

"He's a huge one," the girl says. "Are we just going to
keep him in the house?"

One of the boys turns to Michael. "You do work for us, don't you?"

Another boy presses his face against the glass.

"There goes the special brownies," he says.

"Are you going to save us?" Scott says. "You couldn't save our brownies, can you save us?"

He laughs, and Michael begins to walk around the house. Caroline follows.

Scott yells, "What — is this a bloody sacrifice for the Gods of the Netherworld? Are we the token teenagers dying in this movie? Are you the stuck-up, fuck-faced cops that get eaten by bears later? Yes," he is yelling now. "Yes, I think you are! Assholes."

Michael and Caroline are just going next door.

"I'm waiting for Davis," he says to her. They are in the shadows of another house, alone. He remembers her this summer, tanned. She still has most of it, but the yellow is gone from her hair. It's brown now, and her lips are chapped. But they would be warm. "I don't want us to go into that house by ourselves. We have to get those kids down too."

From next door they hear, in a high falsetto, "Oh save us, oh save us!"

"How long has Scott lived in a bear town?" Caroline asks.

"All his life," he answers.

"You'd think he'd have a little more respect for them," she says.

Her neck looks soft. She has great skin.

"The story of his life," Michael says. "The story of all their lives. I can't imagine growing up here. Nothing to do, a wasteland nine months of the year. We've fallen off the map."

Makes everything not count anymore, doesn't it? This could be outer Mongolia, Michael thinks. None of the rules mattered any more, really. Look at the kids smoking pot in full view of two officers. No one arrested anyone up here for any faults. Nothing counted. Nothing you broke, nothing you stole. Nobody you cheated on. Nobody you kissed, or thought about kissing.

"Okay," she turns to him. "I think we can get the kids down by having them jump onto the roof and then jump over to the next-door neighbour's roof. They have a deck with stairs. And I want that pig's head. We'll use it as a lure."

"Good thinking. All right." They leave the shadows, and he brushes her arm with his arm.

The bear, though, has decided on a different plan. He's investigating the rest of the house. The teenagers long ago crawled up onto the roof, without prodding. Michael sees that the glass on the door is spiderwebbed with breaks. The girl is whimpering, with her hands around the vent. Two boys sit on the roof.

"What are you looking at?" they ask.

"If you're looking for Scott," one of them says, "he's jumped over to the other house and run away."

"Where's the other bear?" Caroline asks. "Did anyone see a second bear?"

"One was enough," a boy says. He smears the black makeup on his face, around his eyes. He looks like a goth raccoon.

As long as Scott's outside, the bears will follow him. Pied Piper with a pig's head, he might soon have a whole train of them after him.

Davis pulls into the driveway on the other side of the house. He gets out of the car. That's how they know the bear hasn't come out of the house. Davis wouldn't get out.

"He's in the house," Michael says.

Davis asks, "Anyone inside?"

"Well, they're on the roof now. No one's injured or anything. Just scared."

"And high," Caroline adds with disdain, as if she never did anything wrong.

"So we need to find Scott Jasper. He's got a fresh pig's head on a stick and the bears are following him around. Hucks needs to get him off the street."

"And then there's the bruno inside," Davis says. "All right, let's go in."

Caroline radioes Hucks to locate Scott and then follows the men cautiously toward the house.

The officers stop at the Jaspers' front door, just inside the walkway, to listen. Of course, the music is overpowering — drums, a dance mix with a girl singing. They can't hear if a bear is in the house or not. They turn on all the lights. The house looks normal — you wouldn't think a bear was in this house. All the furniture is in place. Nothing is disturbed. Yes, a couple of magazines have fallen from the table beside the staircase. And there is snow on the carpet, but couldn't that be from the kids? The officers split up at the stairs, one going into the kitchen. Caroline tries to filter out the noise to listen for bears. She can hear nothing but the bass.

It's ridiculous to even consider making noise to get the bear out of the house. So much noise now the bear wouldn't hear them.

They can't even be sure the bear is in the house.

ANNE HAS TOLD herself that she is coming for Rachel. Coming to take her back home and out of harm's way. She's not afraid of bears — she's afraid of Caroline. She's been looking around now for several blocks, in between houses, in the shadows, for any sign of Caroline or Michael.

When Anne gets within sight of Michael's car, she sees Scott beating on the window, yelling to someone inside. His giant head bobs back and forth over the top of the car. How does he function with blood dripping down his neck?

His fists beat against the glass as if he would shatter it. The fake arms flap like wings beside him. "Open up the door," he is shouting. "Open up the door."

Rachel is inside, she knows. Scott will frighten her. She opens her mouth to call out to Scott, tell him to stop, but he grows more frantic with every moment. He pulls on the broom handle on his back but cannot seem to undo the pig's head and the contraption attached to him.

She sees a white blur come out from behind a camping trailer, moving swiftly past garbage cans and into the street. Scott has jumped onto the back of the car and is trying to escape the bear.

Even at this distance she can see Rachel's hands pressed against the window.

The bear's paws come down hard on the hood of the car. He lifts himself up on two legs and bellows, pressing down on the hood. Scott stands on the trunk. He is seven feet tall himself. The pig's head leers above the whole scene.

Anne cannot move. The bear climbs up on the car — the worst thing that could happen. Scott will not be able to put the car between them anymore, and the bear will move faster than a lumbering boy. She sees another white ghost in between the houses on the right. It ambles across the lawn and watches. It's a smaller bear and will not challenge the larger bear's kill.

Rachel is screaming inside the car; Anne can hear her. She is two houses away and she is running straight at the car. She is waving her arms, she is yelling, she is a living distraction.

Scott finally gets the broom handle untaped from the holster it's been sitting in, and starts to parry and thrust at the bear, who is still on top of the car.

"I have him," he says, his voice shaking. "Get back."

Rachel has succeeded in getting into the front seat and opens one of the doors.

"Mommy!" she screams.

"Get in the car," Anne yells. A paw slashes across the window just as Rachel closes the door.

"Throw the meat over to the side and I'll drive us out of here," she says to Scott.

But he doesn't throw it very far and the bear, when faced with two choices, something dead and something alive, chooses the living thing that smells like fresher meat. The bear leaps from the car.

Anne rushes to the car and jumps in. She shuts the door quickly behind her. Rachel scrabbles onto her lap in tears.

Anne pushes her back. She moves the car in reverse toward the boy and the bear that have become one shape in the night. And she hits the bear with the car, honks the horn, over and over again. She hopes she has not hit Scott, but she doesn't see him any more. She keeps nudging the bear with the bumper.

She doesn't see the other car come up behind her, see her husband take aim and shoot the bear in the back. She only sees the car climb over the bear. Her hands are shaking.

"You've run over him, you've run over him," Rachel says. "Stop, stop."

Michael is now in front of the car and she can't stop the car from moving, or doesn't want to. She pushes and pushes with the car, honking the horn still, crying and not seeing that Michael stands waving at her. "Stop, stop!" he's yelling. "Scott's under the car!"

Michael puts his hands on the hood of the car. Other hands open up the driver's side door to pull Anne away from the steering wheel. She says, "I got him, didn't I?"

Davis says, "You got all of them, Anne."

Davis leads her around to the front of the car where the headlights are shining like spotlights on a white bear with red streaks, and her husband, who stands up. He is clean, completely clean.

Michael looks at her with contempt. "We told you to stop!" he growls.

"I was getting — the bear was on Scott — " she says.

"Why can't you listen to me?" he asks, and while she sees anger for a moment, she also sees fear.

Caroline has Rachel in her arms, and Michael and Davis are rolling the bear out of the way. Davis has to back up the car to do it. To find Scott underneath. Caroline is whispering to Rachel.

"It's all right, it's all right," is what it sounds like, but Anne hears everything wrong. She never listens. She never listens.

She doesn't ask for Rachel, she takes her away. They stand there until the doctor arrives. They take Scott away in the back of an SUV; he's been badly mauled, and his leg is crushed.

Hucks questions Anne. The wind picks up. They move into a car. It muffles all the outside movement, makes every one of Hucks' words sound louder, less comprehensible. Anne doesn't remember where the bear was, where Scott was. She can feel the warmth of Rachel in her arms, on her lap.

Hucks leaves them in the car. Anne stares at the front of the car, imagining the bear, the lurch as the car hit the bear and moved over him. Or Scott. Or something.

The door opens. It is Michael. He climbs in and they drive down the lit street, past the body of the second smaller bear, tranquilized on the snowy lawn next to a For Sale sign. He takes them home, and leaves them there.

WHEN MICHAEL COMES home a few hours later, the house is dark. He flips on the lights but nothing happens. The power is out again. They've burned the bear at the dump. Nothing else to do. The second bear they have in a holding pen. Michael has been shaking all night, can't get out of his head the look on her face through the windshield. She would have run him over. She was mad, crazy mad. He didn't think anything would happen tonight. They had five officers. They had five officers. Five. Five driving around, watching the kids. But no one watches the adults. Or the teenagers. Or the rest of their lives. So much focus on one thing is bound to produce a blind spot. He drops his coat and misses a chair. He can't find his way through the house, and the shadows of the furniture look like moving bears. "Anne?" he calls out. But she doesn't answer him. He can't even use her voice to guide him. He walks forward tentatively through the house, falling and bruising himself on everything he owned.

Alice

Norm Easton

There came a point in that long night
A moment
When it was impossible
To say with any certainty if
We slept
Or moved awake. There was only
A sense
That if sleeping then
We should slumber on, and
If awake
We might never sleep
Content again.

Words to Another Forest Song

Brenda Schmidt

Sometimes a word can be heard over music,
needles twanging twigs
      branches drumming air
           beating on neighbouring trees,
but rarely does its meaning find volume.

Long, this hum — a hum strung like a wood thief's rig
down the throat's slope and wired in the belly
where hewn words slide along fearful of getting caught
in the old growth, in memory so tangled, in the moss-
soft notes rising from the understory.

It is song for the senses. A forest deep reflects
in the eyes of squirrels and, beyond, a clearing slices
pupils into pieces of hard candy light, a humbug
too sharp to suck, too sweet to leave behind.

Even when I fill my mouth with pine needles the taste
  remains
and desire finds a way in — like an ant on a scent trail
it follows no bounds, knows nothing of closed lips.

Here is the whole composition, its elements
wild notes struck; each tone — the rake of bark under bear
  claw,
the plop of water closing in on a frog's escape, the sinking
of marsh marigold pollen — vibrates in the space left
between petals and the surface of what I don't know.

Life After Mining

Brenda Schmidt

It's about needles and moss crushed together, held
in declining light, how it draws a bit of blood,
deepens underfoot the memory of green.

About light and where you'll go
when the place shuts down, is done with you —
some place where roaring is more lion,
less monster,
the glint, teeth instead of steel,
heart, a muscle in a body without ore,
where evening doesn't throw the mine's
shadows back as if it, like you, lost again
its sharp-nailed grip on the structures
you helped build, on the complex now
scabbing the surface of South Main —

about visions of a return to prairie to escape
dreams so rough with the north's rock
your eyes cannot close.
 (You pull lids down and over
the forest and trees poke through skin.
No hurried morning storm,
no unbroken midday plate of sky,
no tears to wash away debris.)

About being remembered for as long
as it takes dynamite to drop a wall of rock,

about a few moments of balance that remain
deeply pressed into the rotting forest floor.

I Like to Wear Dresses

Ivan E. Coyote

I HADN'T BEEN home to the Yukon for over a year, and had been absent from the fold for the last three Christmases. I got a chance to perform in the Longest Night celebration on solstice evening, and a free plane ticket, and I jumped on it.

I could hardly wait to be back: I love how rush hour in Whitehorse is seven cars long, and how nobody even thinks about washing their vehicle until the end of May.

I THINK MY body was actually designed to function in −16°, in the clear blue cold. I like it when the air just starts to sting the backs of my hands, inside my nostrils and the back of my mouth. I love to skate on lakes. It was only December, but I needed a fix, to shake the grey edge of Vancouver off my shoulders.

The thing about going home in the winter is that you have to fly, or risk driving 2200 kilometres in a whiteout, and the plane ride doesn't allow me enough time to adjust.

I always feel twice as weird at Christmas, me with no kids or husband or mortgage, living out of a suitcase most of the time. I forget until I come home how different my life really is. I could chalk it up to being queer, but the truth is, that was just the first straw that drove me from here, separated me from the people and place I came from. But here I was, home, and it felt better than I ever remembered it.

I HADN'T SEEN the boys since September 2001, and they were all a foot taller now. I didn't see them before the show, but I felt them in the audience all the way through my first set. It was intermission, and I scooped them from the foyer and snuck the three of them backstage. Galen was five and wide-eyed, standing dwarfed in front of the timpani drums. Emile was eight, and nonchalant. "I know that," was his cool response to each of my explanations about rigging or scrims or backlights.

And then there was Gabriel. Seven and topped with a crown of brown curls, he was most impressed with the remnants of the smoke-machine fog backstage from the rock star's set. Gabriel has recently taken up the ukelele, his mother had told me on the phone. But he was truly moved by my solo dressing room. "You have your own shower?" he asked me, deeply envious of the perks of my fame, because they slept three to a bed at home. "And so where do you sleep?" he inquired, like he was looking into getting a dressing room of his own as soon as possible.

I noticed Gabriel was wearing just jeans and a T-shirt. Two years ago, on such an occasion, he would have appeared in a velvet skirt, or a long, flowing blouse, and my stomach drops for him. Chris, his mom and one of my fondest loves, told me a few months ago that it has started already. They have started calling him a faggot at school. We knew it would happen, we were just hoping it would happen later. He is allowing it to fold up the little flower inside of him and he now mostly keeps his dresses in the closet and wears them only in the safety and freedom of his own home.

CHRIS TOLD ME later, when the kids were in bed, that Gabriel had initially had on his long, copper velour, lace-up blouse and bell bottoms and pumps when he heard tonight was going to be Uncle Ivan's big show and they were going to the Arts Centre. When he swooped down the stairs to look for his mittens Emile reminded him that Riley (from school) was going to be there, too. Gabriel went back to their room and changed into jeans without a word.

THE NEXT DAY I took him alone (after quite a bit of bickering with his brothers about us needing special time together) to see the second Lord of the Rings movie. I, for one, am scared shitless of the Dark Riders or Ring Wraiths or whatever, and thought maybe it was too scary for a seven-year-old, but he reminded me politely that I had said he could pick. So he, my big old Cheshire Cat grinning dyke buddy Brenda, and I set off for a little queer quality time together, as per the request of his mother.

Gabriel wasted little time. He spent three dollars on those plastic eggs with rings and miniature tea cups in them, bought popcorn with his own money and started asking questions. The first one was brought on by my going to the bathroom, Brenda told me later.

Gabriel leaned across my empty seat to ask her just which washroom I used when out at the movies.

Brenda told Gabriel that, to the best of her knowledge, I utilized the ungendered handicapped facilities whenever possible, so as to avoid confusing anybody in the men's or scaring anybody in the ladies' room.

Gabriel then asked Brenda if she knew for sure if I was a boy or a girl. Gabriel has asked me this himself on several occasions in the past, and each time I explain myself to him as best I can. I'm not sure if he forgets when I go away, or if he just needs to process it all again as a three-, then five-, and now seven-year-old might. Brenda told Gabriel she figured I was technically a girl, but that I had a whole lot of boy in me as well.

WHEN I GOT back to my seat, Brenda brought me up to speed on their conversation. Gabriel's eyes were lit up in recognition and he grabbed my wrist. "I'm just like you, but the reverse." He nodded vigorously and sat up on his heels in his seat. "I'm a boy but I have a little girl in me too." He lowered his voice and looked left, then right. "I like to wear dresses," he confided in his most conspiratorial voice.

My heart felt like it was going to climb out my mouth for the love of him at that moment, and I hugged him over the armrest between us. He was warm and sinewy and he smelled just like his brothers. But he isn't. I don't love them any the less, it's just that I love him more.

"I know you like to wear dresses, Gabriel. I've known you since you were a baby, remember?"

"Since I was inside of my mom? Since Emile was?"

I told him I knew his mom since before she even met his dad, and he shook his head in amazement, like he couldn't fathom a time that long ago.

"Is that why you like to kiss her so much all the time?" he asked loudly, in the not-so-innocent way of babes, and I shushed him because the movie was starting.

IT TURNS OUT that the Two Towers was too scary for both Gabriel and me. At one point he grabbed my hand and bravely whispered, "If this is scaring you too much, I wouldn't mind if you wanted to leave early."

But we stuck it out, and then the three of us drove up Grey Mountain and looked at the tiny, snow-silenced metropolis below us. All the way up the mountain, Brenda and I told Gabriel about our people. About those of us who are boys with girls inside, and girls with boys inside, about all of the beautiful in-betweens and shape-shifters who are his ancestors. Since before even his older brother was in his mom's belly, there were people like us.

Brenda told Gabriel that she was like me, too, a girl with a whole lotta man in her, just it was harder to tell with her on account of her gynormous breasts.

"Yes, they are big," he responded, looking with reverence at her frame, leaning over the shoulder strap of his seat belt and peering into the front seat, his eyes resting on her chest, which has for years been nicknamed by her friends Tyrannosaurus Rack. We told Gabriel that his people have forever been artists and mystics and healers and leaders.

We talked a lot about bullies and their ways. Gabriel blew me away, as seven-year-olds are known to do with

relatives who don't see them every day as all their little
brilliances unfold. He explained that he reckoned his bully
was mean cuz he'd failed grade two twice already, and
his mother maybe drank alcohol when he was still in her
tummy.

I WONDERED, AS Gabriel's fairy godfather should, when
is too soon to warn my young friend about gay bashers,
and how exactly I would go about explaining to a northern
boy-girl a thing as incomprehensible as what happened to
Aaron Webster? Would I just say that people could be really
mean sometimes, and leave out the bit where they found his
baseball-bat-beaten naked body on a trail in the park and
no one saw or heard a thing? What part of the possibilities
would I leave out, to save him from knowing too much
about what I am trying to save him from? He is only, after
all, a little boy.

   I could have cried at the sight of his face, so determined
and sure and aware of his difference. So devoid of shame. I
breathed deep with relief in the knowledge that my presence
in his life will make it easier for him to get through grade
three. I lumped up in the throat for the hope he makes me
feel, now that I'm not the only cross-dresser born in the
Yukon in the family. I will never be alone again. My own
seven-year-old loneliness forged my promise to him to see
that things will, indeed, be different for us as a team.

GUESS WHAT I got Gabriel for Christmas? Earrings, both
dangly and sparkly ones, and fancy French cologne, the same
stuff I wear. It all fits perfectly into the jewellery box he got
from his older brother.

Crow Jane

Philip Adams

JANE PURSED HER lips and blew on the bird. It tucked its head down into the cup of her hand and pressed into the makeshift cradle between her knees. "Oh. Thank God. I didn't kill it." She lowered the bird down onto the gravel road and sat back on her haunches.

Rachel leaned over her sister's shoulder. "Not yet, anyway." She covered her mouth with her hand as if to protect herself and stood up straight. Then, she stepped quickly along the road, batting away the veil of mosquitoes with her thin arms as if it were a cobweb.

"It's still alive," repeated Jane. Sharp stones bit into her shins when she leaned towards the frightened bird. She sat back down on her bum, stretched out her legs and nestled the bird in between them.

"Where the hell are we anyway?" Rachel looked up and down the large valley below them. She had reluctantly agreed to take this side road as a shortcut to a place called

Faro. It was a dotted line on the map and Jane insisted that if it was on the map, then the car should be able to make it. "Oh well — it's a rental," Rachel had finally agreed. There were no guardrails along the road as it snaked through the valley, dropping down and around and then up through a series of tight turns and up up up to where they emerged just at the break in the treeline. There was a long straight stretch of dark brown road ahead of them. They had been arguing about how much time they had wasted by taking the proposed shortcut, so Jane had tromped hard on the gas pedal. She thought the black object on the road was a garbage bag. Then they hit it. And now here they were, stopped in the middle of nowhere. "At least the view is glorious," and Rachel spread her arms out wide to embrace the vista.

RACHEL HAD THOUGHT it a good idea to take this trip together. She had finished her long contract for the oil company, just plain bored of up-start executives who smiled at her as if they had a mouth full of corn syrup, then scowled as soon as the photocopying was done. They had not done anything together since Jane was in the hospital, and so when Rachel asked if she wanted to do something special, her sister said, "Let's go north. It'll be some place new." Rachel had to agree since neither of them had travelled farther than 100 Mile House.

   "It'll be an adventure all right," Rachel had said. "Take your mind off things for awhile." As they laid maps out on the kitchen table that day, Rachel opened her arms wide and basked in the warm glow of their new life. "Me and my sister are gonna drive somewhere new, be some place different, laugh." Now, stranded in the godforsaken Yukon wilderness, she cursed her own hare-brained fantasy. "Adventure is right," she muttered.

"HERE NOW. HERE. It's okay," Jane cooed into the feathers in her hand. She looked at Rachel. "It must have been sick or something. Why was it just lying there?"

Rachel cringed when her sister put her face closer to the bird. "Those things have lice. Live lice crawling all over them. Look. I wouldn't touch it if I were you. They got germs. Don't go kissing it or something now. It isn't a child, Jane." Rachel threw her hands in the air. "But what do I know." She turned toward the car. "Where's the can of Deep Woods?"

THE BIRD WAS heavier than Jane expected. She needed two hands to lift it off the gravel road. She closed her legs, then rested the bird back onto them. She laid the bird's claws out along the V of her thighs, where its head rested near her belly, and blew on its head again. She could smell the coffee still on her breath. In an instant she was back in the parking lot behind the school, nervous, blowing into her clammy hand to see if her breath was strong before heading into the dance. Now the coffee smell was mixed with that of dry dirt and it turned her stomach.

"WHERE'S THE REPELLENT, dammit?" Rachel stomped around the car, put her hand firmly under the door handle and yanked hard. The handle snapped back and the door stayed shut. A chunk of Rachel's fingernail peeled off. "Shitchristgoddamnitshit. What the hell? Jane? Where are the damn keys? Has this thing locked itself again?" She sucked on her fingertip. "Oh for Chrissakes," she muttered and went for the back door.

The coffeed road-dust was now paste in Jane's mouth. Her stomach turned and the sour bile rose in her throat. There was a sketch of a man's face in the dirt beside her leg, his face looking right at her. Mark of the skinny ass who slid up against the bedroom eyes of that blondie who was the nursey-nurse on duty during her bleeding time but they all fall for nurses in white dresses in times of distresses even the ones attending to her fragile womb where his seed had misplanted itself leaving her empty and barren ... and barren and now he ....

"JANE!" RACHEL THUMPED her fist hard against the locked door. Jane jumped at the noise, then quickly constrained the bird's one good wing which thrashed against her thigh. For a brief moment, the bird squirmed hard in her hands, then lay still. Jane settled the bird back down on her outstretched legs and cradled its body as she would a chalice.

"I'm getting eaten alive over here," Rachel shouted. She stormed to the driver's side and wrenched again at the door handle. "Oh right. Good. Right." She cupped her hands around her eyes and pressed her face against the glass. "They're sitting right there on your seat." Her breath fogged the window. "You locked the goddamn keys in the goddamn car again."

"I don't like the noise the car makes when you leave them in the ignition."

AT THE PETROCAN in Trutch two days ago, they had learned how new cars automatically lock their doors. Not the lesson either of them thought they would be having at seven a.m. after a night in the lumpy beds of Pink Mountain Lodge. "Them new c-c-c-cars will do that," said the young man as he rooted up the lock. "These days it's even h-h-h-hard to find a c-c-c-clothes hanger that is stiff enough to p-p-p-pick the lock."

The boy gawked at Rachel when she spoke to him of *the kindness of strangers* and bade him farewell, kissing him and calling him *a sweet boy* before they drove off. Soon the story was reduced to code. *PetroCan k-kisses* became their new catchphrase for everything. For miles they had mocked him. *Always take the k-k-k-keys with you. Either that or we'll just have to p-p-p-pack you along in the b-b-b-backseat for those t-t-t-tricky times when the door just … l-l-l-l-locks itself,* and they had both thumped their heads back against the headrests at the same time, roaring with laughter.

"THEY'RE SITTING RIGHT there on your goddamn seat. How you can be so stupid?"

Jane stayed low on the ground with her head bowed over the raven, searching for another sign of life. She whispered to it, "Gone soon. Mark will be gone. When we get back. Gone." The bird blinked. Jane couldn't look up or over at the face in the dirt. Not now. Saint Mark of The Denial was about to speak. She had stood in awe of his laundry room parable about how the crusty stains on his button jeans were slopped gesso and not Blondie mucous. "She's an artist," he had pleaded. "And so am I. We talk art. What do you want from me?" *Artist* is right.

"JANE?" JANE KEPT her head low and refused to answer her sister. "I'm talking to you. Can't you hear me?" Rachel picked at her broken fingernail. "For Chrissakes, sit up straight. And get up off that filthy road. It is only a dead crow."

"No, it's not dead," Jane yelled out. "And it's a raven."

"Oh, so now it's *not* dead. O-kay. Well, it looks like one dead crow to me. I saw lots of dead starlings on my street once and you can't do anything about them. One big dead crow."

Jane spoke directly to the bird now. "She doesn't know yet. But it's okay now. When he called her a *hoor*, just like Tommy did, I heard him."

"Jane? Are you okay?"

Jane looked straight at her older sister. "Tommy, he called you a *hoor* just like that a *hoor* and you ran him off I saw you both from my window in our white stucco house the one in Kerisdale and then he danced away and hopped the fence Rach…."

"Who?" Rachel was stunned.

"Tommy touched you I saw you you didn't see me you missed seeing me I was there. My Tommy."

"Tommy?" Rachel stopped, twisted her face around, trying to figure out what her sister was talking about.

"Tommy MacGuinn."

"Oh, cut it out, will you? That was years ago. Why do you still hang on to that?"

"I used to. Now, I don't. I just remember things sometimes and then …." Jane grew silent and stroked the black bird's head, impatient with her own tongue. After her time in the hospital, words just tumbled out of her mouth sometimes, all twisted and garbled up. At first her pregnancy had brought her and Mark closer together but then, after the miscarriage, something had slid in between them like a fine linen sheet. She could still feel his body close up against hers but she could not touch his skin.

From where she stood, all Rachel could see was Jane's head on the other side of the car. Rachel stared hard at it, hoping she would turn around. "You are just making that up again. Jane, whatever happened between me and Tommy had nothing to do with you, okay? It was just a stupid, stupid mistake."

"Tommy never called me names," said Jane. "Not like Mark. He used to say nice things to me until I had to get help from the nursey-nurse."

Rachel couldn't bear it when her sister stammered all mixed up and embarrassing.

"Okay, look," she said as she moved towards her sister. "I'm not standing out here in the middle of nowhere, getting eaten alive, while you coo over Tommy or Mark or whoever else you have in that mixed-up brain of yours. I can't think straight for you, I can't sort all these things out in your crazy head. Just leave me alone about it, okay. I said I was sorry a hundred times, no, more than that, a thousand times, and if that isn't enough for you, then you can just take off. Okay? Just take right off."

When Rachel saw the veins on the side of Jane's neck start to pound, she instantly regretted her words. She folded her arms over her chest and dropped her chin down. Her

arms were dotted with tiny rolls of mosquito guts from
where she had wiped them.

IT WAS A long time before either of them moved. Jane picked
at the scales on the raven's large beak and Rachel casually
scraped at the smears of blood with her tapered fingernail.

"Tony's parrot?" said Jane. "You did this? He liked it."
She felt a thudding pressure in her chest. "Chomped down
one day. See?" She turned to face her sister, holding her
finger up. "This scar? Just like that." Her tears made two
glassy lines on her dusty cheeks.

Rachel turned away. This trip north was supposed to
prop her sister back up, raise her spirits, push the *partum*
away, replace it with joy and adventure, and now it was all
collapsing around her. When they were children, Jane would
cry herself to sleep and then wake in the morning with
nothing but sunshine and cheer, as if nothing had happened.
Their mother had loved that about Jane. *Even when times
were tough, you were always so cheerful, Jane. I guess someone
has to be the sullen one, isn't that so, Rachel? Well, at least you
have your good looks to go on.* So when Rachel announced her
plans to marry Tommy, her mother rejoiced but Jane froze
up.

Mommy would hear nothing of how Tommy MacGuinn,
Amos MacGuinn's son from Country Harbour, had reached
out and put his hand right on Jane's chest and kneaded it, as
mysterious to her as when the cat did the same thing. *You
were only 11 at the time, for land's sake, Jane. It's not the big
deal they all make it out to be. This is Rachel's Big Day, Jane,
not yours.* It turned out differently, though. A week before
The Day, Tommy had shown up drunk at their kitchen

door. When Jane answered it, he fell against her, muttering through his gin about how much she looked like her sister. Jane roused the bride-to-be, screaming blue murder for him to keep his filthy hands to himself and that ended that.

JANE TURNED AWAY from the bird and stared out across the valley at the mountains. "I know you … Tommy. Loved him Rach. I'm sorry you lost like that. Scared me."

Rachel turned away. Bugs feasted on her neck. She started to walk back along the road, turned around, and marched right up to her sister sitting on the ground. "Right. You're sorry. Got it. But now what are we going to do, eh?" She wiped the back of her neck. "Well?"

Jane crouched low over the panting bird, its claws clenching and releasing. "There there," she whispered and then started to hum. Rachel took a deep breath, tucked her face down into her blouse to avoid the voracious insects.

Jane turned toward her sister. "PetroCan kisses?"

"Go eff yourself."

"We'll find a way. Look how this bird shakes. See it?" Jane looked up. "Can we wait longer? I don't want to move." She watched as Rachel stomped off down the road toward a large, bald, rock outcrop, watched her pick her way through a thicket of weeds in order to get out onto the promontory. Rachel shaded her eyes and looked over the valley.

Jane felt a thudding in her bones before she heard anything. She sat perfectly still with her ear tuned to the wind, cocking her head back and forth like a robin listening for bugs.

Rachel went further out on the ledge of stones and spread her arms wide as if to receive an answer to her prayers, pleading with the cobalt sky. When she closed her eyes she heard a high-pitched thrumming.

"Jane?" she called out from her dais on the rocks. "What is that?" She waved her arms at the swarm of bugs and darted back to the road, the long stiff weeds whacking at her bare legs.

"Jane. Answer me. Do you hear that?" Her boot caught on a stone and she lunged forward. She flung her arms out to stop her fall, two quick stutter-steps and she was surprised to be still be upright. Jane saw a small black object lift up over the horizon. Rachel scurried up the road towards her.

"PetroCan Kisses," said Jane. Rachel pounced on her, jumping and flapping her arms about as if to get airborne herself. The bird squirmed hard between Jane's legs. One of its claws got stuck in the threads of her jeans. Rachel yelled out to the distant helicopter when it ratcheted on its axis and started away from them up the valley.

"Jane, wave something at them, will you? Where's your jacket? Where is it?"

"Car."

"Give me your shirt. Quick-quick. He's going away." Without waiting for her to unbutton it, Rachel grabbed the collar of her sister's plaid shirt in one hand and a cuff in the other and tugged mercilessly at the material, trying to get it over Jane's head. The bird slid onto the fine dust of the roadbed. Rachel managed to pull the sleeve off, then wrenched at the collar again. The shirt caught under Jane's chin, ripping the two top buttons through the material. "Help me, for God's sake. You're not a vegetable any more, Jane," she shrieked into her sister's ear. Jane stretched her bare arm out to tuck in the bird's wing. The tiny helicopter bumped over the horizon and fell into the green oblivion of the spruce covering the mountain opposite. Mosquitoes dotted Jane's pale shoulders like freckles.

Rachel dropped her sister's sleeve. "He's just going to get help. He saw me. I know it. He's looking for a place to land. Listen." She ran as fast as she could back to her bare rock, cheering on the pilot.

JANE LOOKED UP. "Forgive me." The bird twitched suddenly, squirmed hard away from Jane's hands and scuttled off the road towards the ditch. Everything was happening at once. With one arm out of her shirt, Jane scrambled on her hands and knees towards the escaping bird. The raven stopped, wobbled to its feet, then launched itself straight into the thatch of branches at the roadside. Unable to get airborne, it thrashed through the thicket, tangling and twisting its wings in the unyielding willows. It hopped once more, stopped, then tipped over onto its chest and lay still, held fast in the stiff criss-cross of twigs.

Jane remained on all fours, marvelling at how the bird seemed to be suspended, hanging in the air, almost flying. She crawled over to the thicket, passed by the dead bird, pushed her way through the willows, crept down over the lip of the roadbed, down the long slope clotted with weeds to where the small trees got bigger and taller and the clumps of willows turned to stands of aspen, to where she could stand up straight, to where her knees wouldn't hurt, so that she could hold her head high, watch where she was going, and just go.

Go!

RACHEL COULDN'T SEE Jane at the car any more. She swore, because for damn sure the bird hadn't died yet and she knew that her little sister would still be cradling the fetid thing, moaning and keening and carrying on the way she did. She kicked angrily at ugly stones.

"Jane," she called into the wind. "Jane, stop this. Are you peeing? What?" She spied, then smacked dead, a mosquito on her arm. "Oh, now you're going to ignore me? Jane!" The bug guts dried quickly in the northern air. "Jane!"

She started back towards the car. There was no longer any sound in the hot afternoon sun and the whole valley fell silent. She quickened her pace. Then she saw it. Just the raven lying still, caught in the small trees.

"Fucking crow. Jane?" Now she tore off through the bushes around the car, beating them back in search of a sign. "Jane?" The willows slapped against her legs and tugged at her blouse as she picked her way down through the ditch below the road. A broken stub of buckbrush stabbed straight into her leg and she yelped. When she reached the small clearing, she leaned against a tree trunk to catch her wind. Just above her head were fresh peels of poplar bark with four perfectly dotted punctures in the smooth wood. When she scanned the wide valley, it was all green and still for as far as she could see.

The River

Patti Fraser

IN 1973 I lived on the Fraser River in a little house that needed to be tied to a huge old cottonwood in case of flooding each year when late spring came and the river rose.

I'd step out the door and watch the murky water soak up stretches of the lawn. Each day, the river reached closer and closer to the little house. For hours I'd stand there silently watching the current pull uprooted trees downstream faster than I could have run. The brown water looking like it wasn't even moving.

And that's how life seemed to me, at the time, like some large continent flowing by but appearing as if it wasn't going anywhere.

Then Caleb was born in February of the next year. I had just turned twenty years old. That year, spring breakup came and went and came and went. The ice boomed, echoing in the early morning light. Cracking and heaving like a great live thing just outside the door. It would wake me in the middle of the night in the few hours I managed to sleep.

Then a new cold front would come and the river lay silent and frozen again.

When the ice groaned the newborn would cry. When the river was still, so was Caleb. Every night the same and yet different, just like the river.

My father had taken to coming round occasionally since the baby was born. "To check up on things," he said. He lived a few miles away in one of Prince George's suburbs. His house, like all the rest on McIntyre Crescent, was a cheap insubstantial mimic of the kind that were mushrooming all around the pulpmill city. It was landlocked in every sense of the word. Before coming north, my father had always lived by the sea.

Dad never held Caleb on his visits, or came inside. He would just stick his head in the door at some unexpected time and holler that the steps were clear of ice or the driveway was shoveled and then be on his way. I don't know if he sensed how far from the surface of things I had slipped. Like the river that lay gleaming outside the door, my life seemed to have disappeared and gone completely underground. I strayed little from the house and lived with only the river and his occasional visit for company.

Then in March a train derailed. A carload of lumber slid down the bank across the river from the cottonwood house.

The lumber looked like a pile of matchsticks against the massive cutbanks of the other side.

The next day on one of his visits, my father noted the lumber spill with a beachcomber's glint in his eye.

"It's a find," he said.

"It's too late to cross the river," I answered, uneasy at the way he was eyeing his treasure.

For the next few days, holding Caleb close because it was too cold to put him down, I watched my father drag the lumber by himself, armload by armload, across the rough and dangerous river ice to the little yard of the cottonwood house. His solitary figure hardly visible against the looming walls of the river canyon.

A wave of homesickness swept over me as I stood watching my father tread from one side of the river to the other, the great weight of the newborn holding me fast to this side of the river. And my father, the only adventurer I had ever known, seemed to be disappearing into the blue light of evening as I stood there. Then Caleb cried because it was too cold, and I made myself go into the house.

One night the boom and groans of the river woke me before the baby. I listened to the river changing. Some great mass was about to move. Caleb kept sleeping, his tiny ferocity finally exhausted. I got up and in the moonlight, saw my father still hauling his load across the frozen steppes of the river.

At the back door, I stood frozen and shivering. I yelled at him.

"Stop, why don't you stop. Go home. Just go home."

And he replied, "Just one more trip, that's it, one more." As he carried his load of two-by-fours to the pile scattered across the back yard.

"No, go home!" I demanded, suddenly sick of his presumption, to use this place as his way of disappearing out of his own life.

My father turned to me and I thought he was just about to chuckle, in his way, to let me know nothing was going to stop him. He looked up hard. "It's the only way out of this godforsaken place," he hollered.

"What'd you mean? What do you mean by that!"

"This place, this lousy town. Not a goddamn tree left within five hundred miles of this place except this." Throwing down the last panting armload of two-by-fours. "At least out there," pointing to the crushed edges of ice on the river, "you don't have to ... ya know...."

"Don't have to what?" screaming at him, ragged with rage. "Don't have to what?"

"Take care of anything, right? You don't have to take care of a goddamn thing!"

Afraid he might be right, I said quietly, "You have to go, you can't cross over any more. And you can't keep coming round at all hours, you can't."

My father looked at me hard. "I always thought you'd get out of here."

We both knew then that his last discovery was going to be abandoned. He left the rest of his timber on the other side of the river and got into his truck and drove away.

And for a moment I was lonelier than I had ever been, watching his taillights turn down the dirt road. And then I was glad. Glad to know I didn't have to stand there anymore.

The next night the river started to move.

I didn't see much of my father for some time after that. He started to build a boat in his basement with the lumber that had been retrieved from across the river. The boat was never used since it was too large to get out of the landlocked house. He sold the house that fall and moved back to the coast.

By midwinter, he had a job on a Gulf Island ferry and had sent some money north for me to take a bus down. He was building a house on Denman Island. He wanted me to come and live with him.

That spring, I regarded the river with more care than ever. Holding Caleb close, watching the great rolling currents of brown water creep closer and closer to the house, I knew this was no place to raise a child. The river too large and too swift to forgive any mistaken step.

It was to be my last spring in the cottonwood house. I, too, was moving.

I had realized it was the child who chose the parent, not the parent who chose the child. And together, Caleb and I watched a continent of water flow by, although it seemed as if it wasn't even moving.

Horizon Tells

Nicole Bauberger

The hills' long crossed thighs
seduce the sky's fingers.
Cloud touches earth, and snow
lingers: memory, scent,
and her clothes left behind.

The hill slips into the sky's dress,
wears it awkwardly, more heavily than she.

Even when the clouds don't touch him,
she sends shadows like letters,
distant projections of touch, but still the hill
darkens, marks her motion on his skin.

Then, look, that cloud
leans a tired forehead
into the hill's shoulder.

Elemental tenderness.
Not that they never quarrel but
anyone can see there's something going on.

Let's face it, strong-thighed mountains
are as sexy as any man.
She can't keep her hands off him,
pulls her hair around him like a curtain.
I can't see what they're doing but
the world gets very wet.

Then the curtain parts.
The edge between them clears. It shines.

I don't claim to understand what's going on.
The earth and sky are so much bigger than me
that really, I can barely see them.
I watch this romance like a small child,
my head barely as high as their ankles,

I crouch between the toes of the earth,
swept by the hem of this sky's skirt.

Winter Push-start

Michael Hale

push-starting a car is somehow heroic
in 30 below,
brown bucket jalopies, chariots,
when knees bend and heels dig in
against snow snickering beneath the tire's weight.
A slow, muffled yawn —
choked —
as the engine kicks shit into gear.
Blackened pops! crack in the iced air
and a heart pounds a ta-dah beat —
a winter victory marked with a
"hah!"
jump
and slam.

Buoy

Michael Hale

Gently spent
soaked words wrung from a wet bed,
Epsom questions of detail
         like:

why don't movie baths float imperfect lint and hairs?

I am wound from lint and hairs,
a bristling yarn sphere   floating
here.
A cracked mud hut,
soaking to stay firm,
resolved, replenished, unvexed.

Max And Me

Roy Ness

I LOVE DOGS. I do. Really. When I was a kid all I ever wanted was a dog.

"What would you like for Christmas, Roy?"

"A dog."

"What do want for your birthday, Roy?"

"A dog, please."

My dad would have to explain again patiently. "It would have to spend most of its life inside or tied up. Would that be fair to the dog?"

"But I'd take him down in the bush every day."

DOWN IN THE bush. That's what we called the ravine across the road from our house where I spent most of my free time. Down in the bush made growing up in the suburbs of Toronto bearable. If only I could have a dog of my own, life would be complete. We'd do so much neat stuff together.

I fantasized about the adventures we'd have. I dreamed about getting pinned under a fallen tree. With the little breath I could muster I'd say, "Buddy, go get help, boy." He'd go bounding towards home. He'd have to swim the raging Don River. He'd spot a drowning baby raccoon, take it safely to shore, then race up the hill to our house. He'd bark at my dad, then run towards the ravine and turn around. Again and again he'd bark, run, look back, until finally my dad would say, "Lois, what the hell's wrong with Buddy?" My mother would say, "I think he wants us to follow him. Maybe Roy is pinned under a tree." They'd find me and Buddy would be a hero for saving my life. I'd say, "Dad, thanks for letting me have Buddy." It was pathetic, really — a kid dreaming about being pinned under a tree. Obviously I watched every episode of *Lassie*. My only original contribution to the story was that I'd get to keep the baby raccoon.

The kid I was then would have been horrified to know that one day he would actually hate a dog — hate it enough to want revenge, to inflict pain, even to kill. I'm not proud of it, and I admit I could have handled the whole Max thing a lot better. But mature reflection on painful and embarrassing episodes can provide enlightenment.

My wife and I moved into the Pilot Mountain subdivision just north of Whitehorse in 1982. Like us, most of the people there had young families and were building their own homes. We were called bush hippies by the long-time residents of the Hotsprings Road, but we didn't care. We were living the Yukon dream. We weren't going to tie up our dogs. This wasn't the Toronto suburbs. This was the Yukon, where dogs can run free.

For the first two years I wasn't bothered by dogs because I had one of my own, Weasel, an alpha female who kept all the others at bay. When she died just before our second child was born, I was a stay-at-home dad with a house under construction. I had my hands full, and replacing Weasel was a low priority. I discovered there were advantages to not having a dog. It was nice to look out the window and watch hares playing in the moonlight or the stunning black and grey fox who would regularly trot by.

The trouble was, the neighbourhood dogs had also discovered how nice our place was, especially the garbage, the compost pile and the garden. They began to make trouble for me. I didn't complain to the neighbours because I was sure Weasel had committed her share of property crimes against them. But as time passed, the dogs became bolder and their depredations more serious. I decided on a zero-tolerance approach. Any dog that came by would face a hail of stones and a stream of curses. I discovered the effectiveness of a stick about sixteen inches long. Hurled at high speed end over end it had a greater chance of making painful contact with a retreating butt. I kept a couple of these "dog bullets" at each door. It was about this time that my wife gently suggested, "Maybe the dogs are getting to you, Roy." "No way," I said. "I feel I'm being remarkably tolerant. I love dogs. I always have."

If it hadn't been for Max, the dog skirmishes would have continued at a low level — a mini cold war. But he had a knack for escalating. Max was a handsome brindle-coated

Great Dane who lived down the road. The consummate scavenger, he was sly, resourceful, alert, fast and bold. Thank God he wasn't aggressive with people or he would have been dangerous. Despite his mammoth size, he was an enormous suck, pitifully obsequious when the situation demanded it.

Max was quick to learn my timetable. He knew that the crazy nut at the top of the hill who yelled and threw things did so only during the day. At night Max could have free rein to dig up the garden, tear holes in the greenhouse and gobble up anything resembling food. Then just to rub it in, he'd leave a steaming pile on the doorstep. Its size was titanic, and when it froze you could stub your toe badly (still preferable to meeting it in its unfrozen state). Max seemed to have an unerring sense of timing, knowing when I wasn't looking, when I was out for the day, when I ate and when I slept. I felt as if I was being stalked. I was beginning to hate Max.

Remember, I'm a dog lover. I really am. I tried to focus on his good qualities. I once suggested to his owners that Max, with his size, could pull a sled with ease. I even volunteered to bring my harness down and give him a lesson. The harness was a bit tight, but I was just starting him with a tiny toboggan. I went out in front of him and called. He didn't budge. I called again. He lay down, whining. When I walked toward him he cowered. After twenty minutes he had pulled the sled a total of seven centimetres and that, as far as I know, was the extent of Max's working career.

Our two kids' birthdays are a couple of weeks apart in mid-summer, so we always celebrated with a single party. These were very popular affairs with kids and adults alike, because the garden and greenhouse were at their peak of production. We'd put on a big barbeque and serve mounds of fresh vegetables. The neighbours would walk over to the party, and of course, their dogs would follow. I had built a fence around the lawn and part of the garden to keep our young kids from wandering off. It also kept dogs out, and the whole pack, their noses pressed to the wire, drooled at the sight of all those hot dogs and burgers held in the faltering hands of children — easy pickings if only they could get in.

The entrance to our house is called the mudroom. It's off the kitchen and opens onto the driveway. All summer long, both the inside and outside doors are left open, but there is a screen door to the outside. During one of these parties, I was in the kitchen when I heard a noise in the mudroom. There was Max, reaching his nose up to the shelf where the birthday cake sat with its pink and blue icing. A string of drool hung from his mouth, which was closing in on the cake. "MAX! YOU BASTARD!" I screamed as I ran to the mudroom. Max made for the big hole he had torn in the screen. But his feet couldn't get any purchase on the linoleum and he scrambled like one of those cartoon characters whose legs go a mile a minute but their body stays put. I caught up to him and my foot connected with his sphinctre. That got him moving. Max dove through the screen and got stuck. With me behind him, mad as hell, he ripped the door off its hinges. Up the driveway he ran with the door firmly jammed on his body. Even after Max crested the hill I could see the door over the horizon, still upright, lurching forward and back with each galloping stride.

You might think I'd be angry. After all, Max had wrecked my screen door. But the cake was untouched, the party continued merrily, and I had managed to deliver a satisfying kick to the exit point of all that poo. I felt good. Because don't forget, I'm a dog lover.

Max was a car chaser, too. The road we live on rises gently to our place at the top of the hill. From the turn at the bottom, you can see all the driveway entrances, marked with the yellow of dog pee in the winter and the bright green of urine-fertilized grass in the summer. When any car turned onto our road, dogs appeared at each driveway waiting to give chase. Most people do precisely the wrong thing when a dog dashes out of the brush: they take evasive action, or slow down, or both. This only encourages the dog. You're doing what a prey animal would do. The best approach is to drive as if the dog isn't there. And if the dog misjudges speed and trajectory, or slips at the last moment and ends up under your wheels? My motto is *survival of the fittest*. This might seem a cold and heartless thing for a dog lover to say, but what if you swerve and lose control? That very thing happened to my wife (not on our road) and she ended up killing the dog, demolishing the car, and narrowly escaping death herself.

I got fed up running the gauntlet so I decided to teach Max and the rest of the pack some traffic manners. I first tried yelling, to little effect, so I upped the ante. Before turning onto our road, I would stop and pick up a sizable chunk of ice. Those knobs of frozen slush that fall off the wheel wells of cars work nicely. I'd drive home with my arm extended out the window, ice in hand. At first my aim was poor, but with practice it improved, and a few direct hits encouraged me. Max was the easiest target because he was so big. I started to enjoy the sport of it. You can imagine the challenge. If the dog was on the driver's side it wasn't too difficult, but if it was on the passenger side, I had to lob my missile over the hood while taking into account the dog's motion, the vehicle's speed, and wind resistance. If the dog was small I often couldn't even see my target. With Zen-like discipline, I had to intuit the dog's position. A surprised yelp was often my only proof of success. Remember, too, that I was throwing with my left hand. If this ever becomes an Olympic event I suggest allowing the use of British cars to even the playing field.

Wouldn't you know, as soon as I got good at the sport, the dogs learned not to chase — bummer. I'd turn onto our road, armed as usual, and the dogs would appear at their driveways, ears up and ready for action. But as I approached they would slump with visible disappointment and slouch away. "Oh hell, it's him."

You might consider me cruel, some kind of sadistic monster. I admit I enjoyed it, but only for the challenge. Being hit by a piece of ice doesn't hurt a dog, it only startles him. And consider this: I was the only one doing any teaching, and the dogs, by learning not to chase cars were much less likely to be run over. Who knows how many canine lives I saved? Who is the dog lover here?

My dog problems, like the garden beds dug up and trampled, the garbage strewn, the cold frames smashed, the greenhouse plastic ripped, the irrigation hoses knocked down, the compost pile excavated and electrical extension cords chewed up were mighty annoying. But such vandalism paled to insignificance compared to the evils perpetrated on my moose meat. When we first moved in, we had no sheds or caches to hang meat for curing. I tried various arrangements of tarps, floodlights, a loud radio playing day and night, etc., but none of them worked. When dogs get a whiff of game meat they'll risk death to get some into their stomachs, and Max's stomach was truly bottomless. Nothing could make me rage like finding a big chunk torn out of a quarter of moose or caribou and knowing it was taken by a useless, skulking cur. Maybe it was irrational, but I took it personally.

I admit, Max wasn't the only culprit. I saw dogs that didn't even live in the neighbourhood hanging around waiting for their chance. But Max was by far the worst. Before I built a garage and eventually a shed on stilts, every September was a constant battle with the dogs. More than once I had one in my rifle sights, and only the dog lover in me kept me from squeezing the trigger.

I always bring home the moose skin to tan. One time I had a skin soaking in a barrel of water and wood ash to loosen the hair. I looked out the window to see Max dragging it out of the barrel. Have you ever tried to lift a sodden bull moose skin with the hair still on? I have to use a block and tackle. Max was the Arnold Schwarznegger of the dog world, and damned if my moose meat hadn't helped build his muscles. He would have dragged that skin all the way home if I hadn't had a dog bullet by the door.

After I built the garage onto the house, I thought my problems were solved. But to keep dogs out, one must close

doors securely. One day I'd spent hours carefully cutting
up meat to be made into burger, filling a cooler with about
fifty pounds of it. The next morning the cooler was lying
on its side, licked clean. Max had pushed the door open.
How did I know it was Max? There on the floor was a big
blood-red saucer-sized footprint — a Max footprint. I
was livid. If I had seen him at that moment, I would have
torn out his liver with my teeth. After that, I resolved to be
absolutely scrupulous in making sure all game meat and its
by-products were well out of reach of the dogs, and I did …
until the episode of the foot.

I keep the feet of my moose, to boil and extract the
neatsfoot oil. I use it as a final dressing on finished leather.
I had returned from hunting that day, hung the meat in the
shed, and unloaded the boat and the gear. I didn't finish
until midnight, and as I was coming inside through the
mudroom, I saw I had left the feet there. I didn't have the
energy to go out again, so I decided to chance it for one
night. After all, it was just the feet. It was a balmy night, so
the main door was open, leaving just the screen door — the
rebuilt screen door.

Yes, as you've already guessed, the next morning there
was a big hole in the screen and only three moose feet left. I
don't know why the loss of one moose foot pushed me over
the edge. I knew it was Max. It bore his stamp. It was the
final straw. I'd been pushed exactly one foot too far and I
was about to push back. At that point, I was no longer a dog
lover.

I was so mad I could barely breathe. I went to all the
neighbours who owned dogs and I vented. When I think of it

now I'm embarrassed. I was such an asshole. I told them all the things their dogs had done to me. I told them I was fed to the teeth. The only hint of reason in my ranting was that I did not demand anyone keep their dogs tied up. I told them I could handle my dog problems during the day, but between the hours of seven p.m. and seven a.m. it was open season on dogs at my address. I told them if I saw a dog on my property during those hours it was dead meat — no wounded pets, no expensive vet bills, and no prolonged suffering. I promised it would be quick.

I saved Max's house for last. When I got out of my car, he didn't bark. He went under the porch. He knew. After my spiel I told his owner I was certain Max was the culprit. I was primed for an argument, but the fellow said, "Roy, I can understand your feeling that way. If you have to shoot Max, just call me up and I'll come and collect the body." I was flummoxed. He had taken the wind right out of my sails. Puzzled, I got to my car and looked back at the house. Max was peering out from under the porch. And then it hit me. He hated Max as much as I did, and why not? All that strife with the neighbours, all those trips to the vet to pull porcupine quills, all that expensive dog food disappearing down that slobbering maw. He'd be glad if I shot Max because it would save him the trouble. He wouldn't have to explain it to his kids, because I'd be the villain. I could see he was a kindred spirit — the same kind of dog lover I was.

A couple of weeks went by with no sign of dogs — or neighbours. It was very quiet at my place, even a bit lonely. Then we got a skiff of snow, and the next morning I found a set of big Max footprints around the garage. What to do?

I thought if I could catch Max without anyone knowing, then I could take him out for a walk in the bush and .... I wondered if anyone would notice when he didn't return. If anyone asked me I'd say, "No, I haven't seen Max for some time." My dog problems would be gone — a horrible way for a dog lover to think. But how would I catch him? I'd need some kind of a live trap like the ones they use for problem bears. That would be expensive, though, and building one would be time consuming. Then I looked at the garage. Eureka! My live trap stood right before me. Max wouldn't suspect a thing. After all, he'd snuck in there on other occasions and been rewarded.

It was very simple to rig up. To the outside of the door, I fastened a bungee cord that would swing it closed with enough force to latch it. Then I propped the door open with a stick, to which I tied a string. The string went through a metal eye screwed into the ceiling in the middle of the room. On the end, I tied a nice big meaty bone, high enough that Max would have to reach up to get it. He'd enter through the open door, grab the bait, pull it down, the stick would pop out of the door, the door would swing shut, and Max would be mine.

Imagine my delight when I woke up the next morning to find, guess who, waiting for me in the garage. He knew. His tail quivered as he crawled towards me, pathetic and terrified. I spoke to him kindly as I fastened a strong chain around his neck and gently led him outside. But he knew. I tied him to a tree behind the house. I had to wait until my wife and kids left for work and school. I came back into the house, looked out the window at the grey, dismal

October sky and said, "What a glorious morning. Isn't life wonderful?" They exchanged confused glances. My wife said, "I haven't seen you this happy in weeks." As they piled into the car she said, "The way you're acting, you'd think it was Christmas morning."

In a way it was Christmas, and I was that kid again, a kid who got what he wanted this time — a Christmas puppy. But that kid was no longer innocent, full of sweet, youthful love. Now he was a twisted parody of his former self, full of malice and sadistic fantasy. And the agent of his perversion was tied to a tree out back.

I poured myself a mug of tea, then went out to see my new dog.

"Hi, Max."

He was trembling. "Hi, Roy. Can I go home now?"

"You are home. You're my dog now. How would you like to take a little trip?"

"Where?"

"Far back in the bush, up in the hills to a beautiful place — a resting place."

"I think I'd rather go home."

I thought of what I was about to do. I imagined how I'd feel as I pulled the trigger. I had killed animals before — moose, caribou, ptarmigan, fish — but killing an animal for food and clothing is completely different. Only a sick person enjoys the killing part of it. But I was actually going to relish this. Nobody would ever know. I'd get away with it free and clear and feel not a scrap of remorse.

Then as I sat in front of Max sipping my tea, planning his death, something happened. Maybe the tiny voice of that long lost kid somehow called through the maelstrom of hate in my soul. Maybe I simply realized how pointless revenge is. I could easily justify killing Max. I could tell myself that a lot of other people would have shot him long before things went this far. Whatever the reason, I suddenly knew I couldn't do it.

I had to do something, though. I couldn't just let him go. I wanted him to remember this day for the rest of his life. So I cut a willow switch and I beat him. I don't defend my actions, but then again I could have left this part out or sugar-coated it, called it a necessary evil and the only way to make my point with him. I'm not proud of it, but it sure got his attention.

After that, I felt there was still more to do, and that's when I had an inspired idea. I got paper and a pen and made him sit down and write a letter to his owners, telling them why he should be confined at night. Snivelling and blubbering, this is what he wrote:

Dear Owners,

Please help me. I'm an addict. I can't control my urges. I desperately need your love, understanding, and help to stop my destructive behaviour. When night comes I feel compelled to go to Roy's place and commit heinous crimes. I dig up his garden, smash his greenhouse, and worst of all, steal his moose meat. Roy caught me this time and mercifully let me go, but I'm terribly afraid — afraid that if it happens again he will do horrid things to me. He might seem kind and tolerant to you — even saintly — but I looked into his eyes and saw what's in there. OH! Those eyes! It was like staring into the Abyss.

Please, please, if you love me and you want to keep feeding me expensive dog food, help me. Tie me up at night.

Your loving pet, Max.

P.S. I think he wants to compost me.

I put Max's note into an empty juice can and duct-taped it securely to his collar. Then I grabbed his big loose slobbery lips, one in each hand, and yanked his face up to mine. Max knew if he so much as peeped a protest he was dead meat. It was one of those moments of crystal clear communication across species. Nose to nose, eyeball to eyeball, Max and I shared a wordless conversation. Then I heard a squishing sound and smelled a familiar odour — the distinctive scent of dog poo. You can't imagine my sense of triumph. I had literally scared the shit out of Max. I was finished, so I let him go. Okay, okay, I admit it. I gave him one final kick as he scampered away. Some dog lover.

I never had any more trouble from Max. I guess I convinced him that our place was the abode of the devil. He died several years later of old age (only the good die young). The last time I saw him he was decrepit and feeble. He had followed his owners out for a horse ride, but he couldn't keep up. He was on his way home by himself, stiff in the joints, exhausted, panting heavily. I suppose he hoped he could risk a shortcut through our lot without being seen. I was crouched in the garden, weeding, when I heard his heavy, wheezing, tortured breaths. When I stood, he spotted me, and I could see his thoughts clearly. *(pant, pant) Uh-oh, he sees me. I'd better run. (pant, cough) I can't. (wheeze). I'll just slowly hunch down behind these bushes. (pant, wheeze) Maybe he'll forget I'm here.* It was so pathetic. I could have caught him if both my legs were broken. I said, "I see you, Max. Never mind, just go on home." He got up and continued on his slow painful way. I thought, Should I chase him, just for old time's sake? Should I throw a stick at him? I didn't, and you know why? Because I'm a dog lover.

I am. Really.

The Kill Site

Jerome Stueart

In a place of long grass
and blowing willows,
eagles and ravens
fight over the hide
of a moose lying
beside the river.

A bloody grey sweater,
holed and bored through
by a hundred beaks,
lies tossed to the side
and I ask you if this is an object
of misplaced hunger.

You tell me hunters leave
a sweater draped across the body
to ward off scavenging

until men can return, carve
the carcass, carry it home.

The smell of man
keeps them at bay.

I imagine the sweater holding
the moose's girth in thick
cotton arms at nightfall.
Shadowed beasts and birds
do not disturb
the hunter leaning,
praying, over his kill.

In the morning, yes, I know now,
the sweater will be ravaged
and torn, pocked and ripped,
not because they believe
it is the moose, no

the scavengers see the hunter
has prayed away the kill,
and left them
nothing but a rag
to clean up the site.

Disturbances

Jerome Stueart

At home, everything
is your fault.

You didn't buy the soy
milk and peppers.

You drive too fast
on wet roads.

The laundry is wrinkled
and the towels are damp.

None of your words
make up for the fact

that you killed
the moose and I

became numb
and don't know

how to love the hunter I saw
with his hands inside the steaming body

pulling, pulling
until everything

unravelled.

The End of an Uncertain Grace

Liz Gontard

SUDDENLY, THE YARD was alight. John McTavish got out of bed and went to his window to check who'd set off the motion sensor. A goat stood on the edge of the flowerbed with its head bent to the task of reducing giant, orange poppies to mulch.

John hadn't gone out hunting in years, and he used his .22 to rid the garden of squirrels and magpies. Pests, garden pests. The goat was a bit larger, but he figured one well-aimed bullet would do the trick. He went to his closet and removed the .22 from its soft vinyl case and undid the safety lock. Then, he gently slid open the screen window and raised the barrel of his .22. He focused the scope. The goat's eye glinted in the beam from the porch light. John sharpened his focus until the goat's temple marked the intersection where the crosshairs met.

"This one's for my tulips," he said quietly. He took a breath to steady himself and pulled the trigger.

The goat raised its head and wandered out of the light's beam. The bullet missed its mark and was lost in the darkness.

JOHN HAD MOVED into his daughter Martha's house the previous fall. The move came after his tumble. Martha called it a fall, but John looked on as more of a stumble. He stumbled over his feet. However, the gash that resulted from where his forehead had connected with the coffee table was impressive and left him with a scar that ran from the outer edge of his left eyebrow up towards the centre of his forehead.

When he moved in with his daughter, he'd planted garlic bulbs in the weedy patches of earth she referred to as her garden and various flower bulbs in beds under the windows. He had glorious plans for his garden. The first garden in the four years since he'd started living in apartments after Peggy, Martha's mother, had died.

The goats had been garden pests from the day Martha had brought the three of them home from the animal shelter. She wasn't interested in dogs or cats or even hamsters. She wanted the goats. She wanted them for milk. She intended to make cheese. But Martha rarely had time to milk the goats and they spent most of their summer destroying John's flowerbeds and vegetable garden.

On their first night, they tore apart his prized tulips, the ones he grew from the bulbs special-ordered from a prizewinning grower in Holland. Martha apologized and promised to tether them overnight, but the goats soon learned to chew through the ropes that restricted their roaming, and often escaped to wreak havoc on various parts of John's garden. By July, John's vegetable garden had been subjected to irreparable damage: his snow peas reduced to shredded stalks of green and his kale mowed down one Sunday afternoon in less than the half-hour it took to catch the escaped goats. His cabbages — he didn't like to think of the cabbages very much. They had been doing so well. One red cabbage in particular had grown to be two feet in diameter, and he had planned on entering it in the annual Finlayson Summer Agricultural Fair. But one night the goats escaped, and in the morning, John added the few remaining red leaves to the layers of his compost pile. With the fair nearing, the only flowers he'd managed to protect from the goats' ravaging antics were his giant poppies.

John considered himself to be a gentle man. A man who rarely acted without first carefully thinking through his actions. He waited for the pedestrian signal before crossing at the crosswalk, even when there wasn't any traffic. His gentle demeanour and careful nature had helped him adjust to the changes that had taken place in his life since "the fall;" he'd taken the diagnosis of the big "P" with neither shock nor theatrics. He knew he was aging, and illness was a part of that process. He'd adjusted equally well to living with his daughter. He'd accepted the single bed in his daughter's spare room, even though he'd left behind a double bed in his own apartment. He'd adjusted to her brown-rice way of eating and her concern for his health. He had taken it all in stride. He had, in his thoughtful, quiet way, been enjoying his retirement in the country.

However, when John saw the goat standing among the last remaining beauty of his garden, the giant poppies that he'd worked so hard to protect (he'd even gone as far as to build a chicken-wire fence around the poppy bed), he felt an anger rise inside him. He had adjusted to all the changes so far, but he could no longer acquiesce to the invasion of the goats.

JOHN WOKE TO the sounds of Martha moving around downstairs in the kitchen. The utensil drawer slammed shut, the pantry door creaked, her slippers made a whooshing sound as she dragged her feet across the linoleum. When she was young, he had always impressed upon her the importance of raising her feet when she walked, but at thirty-four years old, Martha continued to drag her heels. He waited for the sound of the coffee grinder and didn't hear it. That absence of sound meant a breakfast of fibre flakes, prunes, yogourt, and a long sit for John in the bathroom afterwards.

"Not this morning," he said to himself. He rolled out of bed, his back a little stiff, and got dressed. As he reached for the doorknob, he noticed that his hand trembled.

In the kitchen, Martha squatted in front of the open fridge with its contents spread on the floor.

"Good morning," John said. "What are you looking for in there?"

"I can't find the bacon," she replied. "I picked up Harold's groceries yesterday when I got ours, and I can find everything else except the bacon. You haven't seen it, have you?"

"No. Don't think I went in there after we put the groceries away. In fact, I don't remember seeing any bacon at all. Are you supposed to drop his groceries off on the way to work today?"

"As usual, you know."

John looked around the kitchen and saw the teapot sitting on the counter.

"No coffee this morning?"

"No, it's Wednesday."

"Right. Wednesday. When can I drink coffee?"

"We agreed on Sunday and Thursday, remember?"

"Oh, yes. Twice a week. I remember."

"There's tea in the pot. Ginger-peach."

"Hmmm, yes."

"You'll probably want some honey in it."

"Yes, I'll do that," he said and turned towards the teapot on the counter.

"Oh, I can't find it anywhere. I probably left it at the store."

"Guess you'll just have to pick up some on your way to work."

"I don't think I've got the time."

"You could leave a little early. I'll wash up."

"Yeah, I suppose." She paused. "How are the shakes this morning?"

"Fine, fine. Nothing more than usual."

"Don't forget your appointment with Dr. Stinler this afternoon. You catch the bus at three and call me when you want me to pick you up."

"I won't forget," John affirmed. "Shouldn't you be on your way?"

"Yeah, soon. You know, I thought I heard a shot last night. You didn't hear anything, did you?"

"I think I heard a car backfire near our end of the road. It was late. Probably the Jessup's boy. His muffler needs a patch or two," he said as poured himself a cup of tea.

JOHN WAITED UNTIL he heard her car turn at the end of the driveway. He took his cup to the sink and poured out the cooled contents. Again he noticed how his hand trembled a little more than usual. He rubbed his hands together and that seemed to help some. He shook his arms over his head to get the blood flowing and the trembling became hardly noticeable.

"The ones who succumb are those who don't do anything about it," he said. "Now, time for breakfast."

Most mornings he abided by Martha's healthy diet, but once in a while he liked a good fry-up. He kept everything he needed for his occasional indulgences in a small leather suitcase at the back of the closet in his room. Inside the suitcase there was a bag of ground coffee, a carton of eggs and a loaf of white bread. For snacks he had some potato chips, Cheezies and beer nuts. For extra special occasions there were cigarillos. Those he smoked on holidays like Christmas, Easter and Canada Day.

He collected the eggs, bread and coffee from the closet, then went over to his bed and stuck his hand between the mattress and box spring and pulled out Martha's missing pack of bacon. He returned to the kitchen, opened the windows and back door and began to make himself breakfast. He hummed as he cracked two eggs into the frying pan that was slick with bacon fat.

WHEN HE FINISHED eating, he went into the living room and opened the front door. He needed a good breeze through the house to get rid of the bacon smell. He placed the garbage in the fireplace and set it alight, letting the fat from the bacon packaging instigate an acrid fire that quickly consumed the egg carton. As the evidence burned in the living room, John flushed the coffee grounds down the toilet. Now there were only the dishes and, once he'd washed those, Martha would never know. On his way back to the kitchen, he stopped suddenly in the doorway. One of Martha's goats stood on top of the kitchen table and was gnawing on a place mat.

"You bugger," John said. His right hand began to tremble.

The goat continued to chew.

John's body tensed. The anger he felt the night before, as he watched the goat eat his poppies, returned. He quickly made his way up the stairs to his bedroom and again removed his .22 from its soft vinyl case. He removed the safety and loaded the chamber. He placed a handful of bullets in his pocket. His hand began to tremble, but he ignored it.

When John returned to the kitchen, all three goats were standing there. The one on the table had begun to scrape layers from the table top; the other two were busy destroying the recycling box and its contents. John raised the .22 to his shoulder and levelled the barrel at the goat eating the table. The animal's yellow teeth grated on the wood.

"This one's for my poppies," he said. The barrel moved back and forth from the target. John took a breath to steady himself. Still, the barrel wavered. He placed his finger on the trigger. The barrel seemed to grow even less steady. He closed his eyes and counted to three. When he opened his eyes the barrel was pointing at the stove. The goat pulled chunks from the table. John raised the barrel again, closed his eyes, counted to five, tensed his finger on the trigger, opened his eyes, sighted the goat and shot. The bullet disappeared into the floral-patterned wallpaper. The goat remained standing. It raised its tail. Brown pellets rained from its anus and fell clip-clop on the table. The other goats ripped noisily through the blue plastic of the recycling box.

John reached into his pocket and pulled out a bullet. His entire forearm was shaking. He tried to load the chamber, but dropped the bullet. It landed on the linoleum. He reached into his pocket again and pulled out another bullet. This one he managed to load.

He leaned his shoulder against the door frame for support and that relieved some of the shaking. He raised his rifle, sighted the goat's head and pulled the trigger. The goat let out a squeal and leapt from the table. It looked around, its eyes wide with shock. Blood poured from the small hole below its rib cage. A pool of blood swelled on the floor. The goat looked around and bolted for the open door, leaving a glossy stream of red in its wake.

"Damn," John said. He stepped away from the door frame and made his way past the two other goats and outside to the back porch. He had planned for one clean shot. Now, he had to chase after the animal to finish it off.

OUTSIDE, THE GOAT was nowhere to be seen, but John followed the trail of blood from the porch, past the flowerbed, along the length of the house where he caught sight of the goat heading into the trees at the far end of the yard. He quickened his pace and came upon the goat collapsed under a hemlock. The goat whined, its white coat soaked a deep burgundy.

John tried to raise his rifle, but he seemed to have no strength left in his arm. He lowered himself to the ground and lay flat. He laid the rifle in front of himself, the muzzle pointed at the goat. He loaded the chamber, put all his weight on the butt of the rifle to raise the barrel, and fired.

The goat let out a wail as the bullet hit it in the leg. John took the three remaining bullets out of his pocket and spread them on the grass. His fingers quivered as he reloaded. The bullet's casing clinked inside the rifle's steel chamber. He fired. The goat let out a scream as the bullet hit. John fumbled with the second-last bullet. The animal's irregular breathing was loud in his ears. The bullet slipped from his fingers, but he recovered it and slid it into the chamber. He steadied the barrel and fired. The shot was lost in the forest. The goat continued to whine.

Holding his breath, he grabbed the last bullet and lifted it above the open chamber. His hand was struck by a severe spasm, and he let the bullet fall. It landed backwards in the chamber.

John laid down his rifle and pushed himself to his feet. His back felt as stiff as when he'd woken. He headed towards the garden shed. As he looked around the dim shed, he suddenly felt queasy. His options were few. The shovel wasn't heavy enough, and he didn't want to think about using the pitchfork.

The sledgehammer connected with a muted thud against the goat's skull. John left it on the ground beside the goat and walked slowly towards the house to get a garbage bag. His tremors had passed, but he felt very cold and wanted badly for a cup of something hot. Even one of Martha's teas would be all right. When he reached the open back door, he was overcome by the sight of the disaster in the kitchen. The two goats had returned to the yard, but their teeth marks and droppings were on just about every surface. John sat down in the doorway and began to cry. He sat there for a long time, his body heavy with sobs. He knew he had to clean everything up. He just didn't know where to start and when it would end.

Black Roost

Michael Reynolds

This tree preens
the dusk air black.

Rough-hewn coos crack
and rattle the limbs' yeared rings.
Thick-beaked chatter,
like the clack and clatter
of a horrendous typewriter.
Winged characters flap
then fold against cold,
turning into themselves
like blind, still
eyes

until dawn,
when the black spruce
falls apart to the sky.

Raven: first voice

Michael Reynolds

crack-coughed dawn come flied in
feathered from shit roost — black spruce

whoosh   whoosh   whoosh

light-on-a-roof on-a-lampstand — cry
throa'to-th'sky throa'to-th'sky
catch-in-my-throat

MINE! MINE! MINE!

split bag gristle rip
stick in my craw

pluck-th'dead pick-th'bone
't'll-never-go-home

Yellowlegs

Al Pope

PAUL WEARS AN old man's clothes: clean, pressed cotton shirt, wide at the bottom, grey polyester pants, wide at the top. Tan loafers he doesn't have to bend to lace up. Thick bifocals that distort his eyes. In his hands is a homemade basket, fashioned from unpeeled branches of willow, crude, but with a certain coarse beauty. It's the first one he's ever made, and he'd like to share it with someone. Hearing footsteps, he looks up, expecting his daughter, who taught him this skill.

"Grampa, hey grampa, lookit. Socks." Paul looks down with mixed love and annoyance. Lonnie could be himself at four years old. He has the same chubby face, the same ruddy complexion, the same stout build. But his clothes: he wears baggy shorts that hang to his knees, a T-shirt three sizes too big. Why does Irene let him dress like this? Don't we send him nice clothes every Christmas, birthdays? It's not like he has nothing to wear.

The boy is holding up an armful of dirty socks, some of them so foul that Paul is certain they will have to be thrown out. It's disgusting, unhealthy, he shouldn't have them so close to his face like that.

"Where did you get those, Lonnie, they're filthy. Here, put them in here." He holds out the basket and the boy cheerfully dumps in the socks.

"Under my bed," he says proudly.

What kind of housekeeping is that? Is that why Dan left? Paul scowls at himself. Some things you shouldn't think.

He turns at the sound of wooden-soled sandals on the plank floor.

"Lonnie, did you clean out under your — oh there you are. Morning, Dad." Irene is wearing that old hippie dress, third day in a row, but with some kind of embroidered blouse, and a silly-looking necklace, all made of different beads. Like something you'd give a kid for dress-up. For God's sake, she's nearly forty. Her too we send nice clothes. She has such a beautiful face, she could be lovely if she'd try. She could look just like her mother at that age. He hands her the basket.

"Oh, and your *basket*. Dad, it's *beautiful*. It's perfect. It took me ages to get them this good."

Paul just grunts. He doesn't want to talk about the basket now. It's soiled by those socks. They're stupid baskets anyway, something Lonnie could do. He remembers baskets from his childhood, proper Ukrainian baskets, neatly built out of something clean-looking, colourful, not like this with the bark still on.

"I'll just dump these in the laundry and bring back the basket," Irene says. "Why don't you two go and see if Grandma's got some breakfast ready."

There's something funny about the way she speaks, as if she's forcing herself to be cheerful. Does she think Paul cares about the stupid basket? He's not a child, he wants to say, but she's gone. By now, Paul is beginning to wish he was back in Toronto.

"Come on," he tells the boy. "Let's get something to eat."

The kitchen is warm, and smells of coffee and hot cooking oil. The morning sun lights up the table by the window. Paul admires the red highlights in the oak surface, the neatness of the joinery. It's not the table that was here before. Dan must have built it. Before he left. Ada is flipping pancakes at the woodstove.

"Well, good morning, Lonnie," she says, crouching, arms extended for a hug. Ada is slim and energetic. Like a young woman, except for her skin. She's as old as Paul, but she hasn't accepted it yet. Hasn't had to. "I'm just learning to use Mommy's stove. I haven't cooked on one of these in years. Did you make your bed?"

"Not yet." Lonnie looks straight at the pancakes. "What's for breakfast?"

"Porridge."

"Ha, Gramma, it is not, it's pancakes."

"Why'd you ask then? They'll be ready in five minutes. Why don't you go and make your bed while you wait?" But the boy is already on his way to the bookshelf in the dining area. He pulls out a picture book and takes it to Paul, who is sitting at the table.

"Will you read this to me, Grampa?"

"Let's see it then." Paul tips his head back to read the title. "*The Little Red Hen.* Why, I used to read this to your mom when she was a little girl." Lonnie ignores this. He's looking in the book, waiting for Grampa to open it. First, Paul opens his arms to welcome the child onto his lap. "Let's see if it's changed any."

Deeply absorbed in the warm feeling of holding the boy and reading to him, Paul doesn't notice when Irene comes, places the empty basket on the table, and goes to help with breakfast. Just as he's reading the last sentence, closing the book on the words, "and that's just what she did," two plates of steaming pancakes appear.

"Thanks, Irene," he says, as Lonnie jumps down. Ada comes with two more plates, and Irene goes back for coffee and mugs.

"Did you see Dad's basket, Mom?"

"*This* basket? Oh, Paul, it's lovely. I thought this was one of yours, Irene."

Paul glances up. There's something he likes about the way his own rough basket contrasts with the fine workmanship of the table. He'd like to say so, but it would mean talking about Dan. He doesn't know how to do that yet. Let her bring that up herself.

"It's not right," he says. "Look at it. It sits crooked."

"Dad, they all sit crooked. They're rustic baskets."

Paul just grunts. Let it pass. But Irene is clearly put out. She sighs, and tosses her hair, and for a moment Paul is in the old kitchen in Streetsville. The sun lights the red Formica table, the smell of cooking comes from an old electric stove. His infant daughter tosses her head in defiance. Tears well up in his eyes.

"What's the matter, Grampa? You crying?"

"It's just my eyes watering, son. Happens when you get old. I just need some fresh air." Trusting, Lonnie goes back to his pancakes, but Paul is painfully aware of two pairs of eyes that follow him as he lurches from his chair, and tries to hurry from the room. Blinded by the drops that build up behind his glasses, he stumbles into the kitchen cabinet on the way past, knocking over a Corel plate, which rattles noisily on the floor but doesn't break.

"Goddamn bifocals," he says as he blunders out the back door. "Can't see a goddamn thing." In the cluttered porch his breath turns to mist. These Yukon mornings. You'd never think it was August. He falters. How can he go back into the kitchen for his jacket? Looking around he sees an old mackinaw of Dan's, hanging on a nail. The heavy fabric is cold, and he shivers putting it on. He stands on the doorstep, not knowing what to do. His eyes are hot. He takes off his glasses and wipes them on the jacket. In the blur of his vision, the play of pale sunlight and shadow through the spruce trees breaks up the river mist into patches of gold and silver.

Paul loves this place. He remembers the summer when he and Ada came to help build the house, the four of them living together in the old cabin. Paul was strong then, not so long ago, and helpful when there was a heavy timber to lift, a spike to drive. But it was Dan, always deft-fingered, who chiselled out the dovetails, who engineered the raising of the posts, the fitting of the beams.

Paul's still shivering in the chilled mackinaw. Going to have to do something to keep warm. There's an axe and a chopping block by the door, and a stack of pine logs waiting to be split. The axe is a good one, he can tell, even as he pulls it from the block. As he tests the heft and balance in his hands, moving his fingers around to keep them from stiffening on the cold wood, he thinks, yes, this is the kind of axe Dan would have. Good edge, too.

Setting a small log on the chopping block, he tries a couple of feints with the axe to get the distance right, and then swings. It cleaves the wood easily and as he works he finds himself wishing Dan was here to see him, still capable of swinging an axe, by God. That bastard. A man with a wife and family, thinks he can just go running off. No sense of responsibility. But then, who knows? A man doesn't just leave for no reason.

Angry at himself for the treacherous thought, Paul swings too hard. He splits the log, but drives the axe deep into the chopping block, where it sticks. Pain shoots through his arm and stabs at his back. At that moment the door opens and Irene steps out.

"Dad, are you all right?"

Paul desperately wants to say yes, I'm fine, but he can't speak right away. He steadies himself against the axe handle, breathing hard. She comes and puts her hands on his shoulders. "Dad, are you going to be all right?"

"I'll be okay. In a minute," he tells her. And he will, it was just the shock; he's starting to recover already. After a minute or two he straightens up and says, "Thanks."

"For what?"

"Not telling me I shouldn't be chopping wood."

"Looks like it was going all right for a while there," she says, looking at the split wood lying all around. Her casual tone sounds forced.

"Give me your arm and let's walk around a bit till I get my legs back."

They take the trail that runs down by the river. It leads through a grassy clearing and then narrows to single file. Paul lets go of Irene's arm and steps out ahead. He's doing fine now, though painfully conscious of his old man's bowlegged gait. The rapids here play loudly on the rocks. Irene speaks over the noise.

"You gave me a scare there. What happened?"

"I was thinking about you and Dan, and I drove that axe into the stump so hard I damn near shattered my arm." A flash of blue swoops over the water. "Look, a kingfisher."

"Beautiful, aren't they?" She kicks a stone. The bird swoops again. "That's what I wanted to talk to you about."

"Kingfishers?"

"Don't be cute, okay, Dad? I've been trying to talk to you since you got here. You change the subject, you make jokes. It's hard enough to talk about as it is."

They come to a place along the river where the edge of the tangled spruce forest sweeps back from the bank, giving way to willow bushes, and then a strip of sandy beach. He turns to face her, taking a breath.

"Tell me what?" he says.

"Dan left me because he's gay." The words come out all at once, as if from a jug, tipped too far. Paul takes a breath. He has to respond. What to say?

"A married man?" he says. "A father?"

"I know. But I guess it happens. I didn't have a clue, you know? I mean, one night he just came home and...."

Mechanically, Paul sits down on a broad stump at the edge of the sand. A bird, some kind of sandpiper, dashes onto the beach on spindly legs. Surprised to find company, it spreads its wings and glides across the water, piping a distress signal. Irene comes and sits down. The sandpiper darts back and forth on the far shore.

"Frantic little bird," says Paul.

"Yellowlegs," says Irene. "They're ground-nesters. She'll be giving us the broken-wing treatment next."

"Does your mother know?"

"Yeah. She knows."

As they sit watching the bird, Paul's remembering. If he could forget, he would.

He and Dan, tanned and strong from weeks of building, working all day to erect the ridge timber of the new house. Their backs and arms strained against the levers as they jacked up the beam and set the chokers. Keeping their weight on the chain-blocks, they kept their rhythm with flashes of eye contact as they manoeuvred the timber to the tops of the posts, twenty feet above their heads. The beam swayed slowly as they scrambled up the scaffold to push it into place. Paul's breathing was laboured as he hurried back down to slack off the chains, while Dan walked the ridge beam, tapping it here and there with a sledge to coax the dovetails together. At the last second the timber settled with a clunk, and Paul's heart stopped as Dan swayed to keep his balance, and then, silhouetted against the sky, the sun trapped in his blond mop, he flashed a thumbs-up.

"*Yeah*. Fits like Fred and Ginger."

The women were still busy with supper, and the two men stood outside the cabin, drinking beer, ice-cold from the river. Irene stuck her head out the door.

"Sauna's lit, you know. Should be nice and hot. There's just time for a sweat before supper."

The sauna was dim after the hard afternoon sun. Easing his skin onto the hot cedar bench, Paul could feel the aches beginning to flow out of him. Dan bent to open the stove door.

"You're not getting it hotter in here, are you?" Paul protested, laughing.

"Damn right. Hotter the better."

When the sweat streamed from them and breath came short, Dan took the tin dipper and threw water on the rocks. A thick wave of steam drove them out the door, down the path, and into the cold river.

Paul remembers that steam rose from Dan's shoulders as they came whooping and laughing back to the sauna. He remembers the feel of the rocky ground on his bare feet, the aspens along the path shimmering, the feel of something huge and inexpressible till Dan turned around at the door and Paul, without realizing what he was about to do, enfolded his friend in a great bear hug.

When Paul stepped back, grinning, he saw the puzzled look on Dan's face, and realized what he'd done. Two naked men. The river faded to silence behind him as he and Dan held each other's eyes. How long? A second, five seconds maybe? Long enough to know, without looking down, for he dare not, that he was pointing obscenely at Dan. Long enough to see that Dan had noticed, that he wasn't looking away. It was long enough for Paul to live the minutes that could so easily follow, minutes in which his hands might wander down Dan's cheeks, ghostly as a spider's web across a path, down his neck to his chest, where Paul could imagine just the gentle roll of thumb and forefinger that would make breath catch, head arch back, exposing stretched neck muscles to the touch of his lips while his hands slid down and around to explore the hard sides of those young hips. Long enough almost to feel a young man's silky beard on his face, to taste the salt on his lips, before Dan broke away, and, turning without a word, with only a sad, ironic smile, went through the door and into the sauna.

For another immeasurable moment Paul stood outside the sauna, his face burning, his breathing shallow, stunned by shame and embarrassment. How could this happen? How did such a thing come over me, I'm not queer, for God's sake. *I'm not queer.* He wanted to yank the door open and shout it at Dan. He wanted to run away, never have to face Dan again. He thought of marching back to the cabin, whisking his wife off to the bedroom, proving his manhood right on the spot, saying see, see, it didn't mean anything, it was a random hard-on, a manly embrace. Like *football players*, for Chrissakes. Like those European guys, Greeks. No, not

Greeks, Jesus. Spanish or something, *manly guys*, that hug
each other all the time, and it doesn't mean a thing. *It doesn't
mean a goddamn thing.*

AFTER A MINUTE the yellowlegs flies away, skimming low
over the water. Paul's reliving his shame, plumbing the
depths of his capacity for guilt. He put this whole thing out
of his head years ago. Sort of. But now he has a new burden
of guilt. Because Paul knew. Long before the kid was born,
when Irene and Dan were still young, before they built this
dream — family, home, jobs, lives spun together symmetric
as an egg — Paul had seen the thing that would split them
in two. But he never told, because what could he have said? I
made advances to your husband and he took several seconds
to decline? Right. And now? If ever anything is to be said,
this is the time. But what? For God's sake, what? Paul knows
there is something he should say even now. Something
which, left unsaid, will stand like a wall forever between him
and his daughter, a wall which no one but Paul will be able
to see.

So how the hell long is forever, anyway? Paul stands up.
"I'm getting cold sitting here," he says, "let's go back."

"It's all right, Dad. We're doing okay, me and Lonnie.
You know?"

Paul turns to look at her. He doesn't know what to say.
He wasn't really thinking about her at all. He tries now
to imagine her situation, but it's beyond him. He uncoils
himself, getting gracelessly to his feet, and turns to offer
Irene a hand. In the touch of her fingers, the carefully

measured weight she places on his arm, he feels the affection she has for him. It's enough. Or it'll have to do, at any rate.

At the house, he notices the basket, lying in the sandbox. Lonnie's already had time to drag it outside, play with it, and then lose interest. Paul picks it up, shakes away the sand, and turns to Irene.

"Kids these days," he says. "No respect."

"That's what you said thirty years ago."

"Was it? Must have been true then too."

Paul takes the basket and goes inside. Passing through the kitchen, he drops the basket on the table. He was going to speak to the boy about carelessness, responsibility, but why bother? Who listens?

Conjectures of a Northern Journeyman

Gregory Heming

FALL WIND IS cream, thicker than summer's, and on it float
a hundred or more Canada geese. All at once, as if prompted
by a click of the fingers, they drop into the Alsek valley
like a breathing arrow. Cutting diagonally across the pale
face of Profile Mountain and spreading out over the gold-
braided channel of the Dezadeash River, their finely-tuned
flight sputters. They break apart, circle, but do not land. In
a moment they put right, draw together beneath the heavy
September sky and push south.

Lying on brittle auburn grass in the meadow, I watch
them until they are but a thin grey line drawn right to left
through the most distant peaks. My mind drifts to memories
of my father and the fields of geese he would watch from the
porch of his Colorado home. With tired eyes peeking through
the dim haze of old age he would count these birds as best he

could, call me, and weave a story. Migrating birds became a way of connecting our two worlds, wings touching timeless air, moving along memories as rich as morning chatter, as real as tears.

WE DEFINE OURSELVES through our stories. We tell these stories to others. And we enter other's lives as listeners to their stories. Like fall leaves on this valley floor, detached and light in the wind, our stories scatter our personal histories. They are woven from our experience with our natural and cultural landscapes, blended without spatial or temporal boundaries. In stories we tap into an inheritable ecological reckoning — a stream of very old consciousness — merging us with our place. Recounting stories I have heard from others living in this valley adds some lively polish to my journey here, but they will not be my stories. The proper study of this place will take place over time, and will emerge from the stories that I will tell.

This meadow I stretch out in today, and the mountains that hold it in, are much older and larger than I can immediately comprehend. Given time, however, my memory of them will become deep and wide. Today, in this meadow, land and memory travel together over bold grey granite and big ice. It is as if I am both in this place and of this place. Living memory — the stuff of stories — is informed and formed of climate and geography. This ecological nitty-gritty influences the way we talk and what we talk about. And it is what sculpts the brain in which we think — our human mind. I find some comfort in knowing how deeply I am captured in this place. Yet there also remains uneasiness in this knowledge, for I know as well that, without choice, this place will become what I imagine it to be. Place and imagination run along the same ground.

This is my fifth year living at the mouth of a great antediluvian valley. It is a valley spur carved from the elongated Shakwak Trench. Directly to the west rise the highest coastal mountains in the world — the St. Elias. From my cabin I can look south into the narrowing Alsek valley, a fragile and sharp granite trough through which the rivers and the runoff in the trench drain. The water here is filtered by the open boreal forest of black spruce and balsam poplar that matures in the shallow dank soil that almost floats on permafrost.

Here I have watched grizzlies saunter through stiff spring willow near Buffalo Rock on the eastern edge of the valley, their dark humps bent over arctic ground squirrel holes that look as if they have been punched into the valley floor. In early spring and late fall, moose and coyote travel identical pathways north out of the valley. Wolves, in seeming defiance of the arctic winter, wait until late December to break free of this cold grey valley, their bold paw prints, pressed hard into the frozen snowpack, remain there as maps of their necessary journey. I sense the inherited dependence these animals have on each other, and they live inside me as both memory and myth. This is both humbling and tragic to me. As memory and myth, we allow some wild creatures transformative powers far beyond their primitive ones. We begin to see their complex evolutionary dependence as savagery, and they enter our vocabulary as synonymous with all that is dark, evil, or confrontational. We have, I am afraid, forgotten what these animals, in fact, mean.

My journey here in southwestern Yukon has been a resolute descent into its natural and cultural past. It has demanded of me that I nurture a deep sense of solitude, deeper perhaps than at any time in my life. I am held to this place by dark and remarkable winters followed always by brilliant flashes of summer. As seasons pass, my insistence on imposing a human order on the nonhuman world has forfeited its grip. On winter nights, companioned by little more than a copper oil lantern, I have begun to forge some understanding of the connection between landscape and mindscape, and ultimately, between wisdom and wilderness.

During long walks along Bear Creek with my old dog Joe, I have begun to painstakingly piece together the notion that the instrument of morality is imagination, and much of what we imagine is genetic. I see our ability to be wise as the result of our multimillion-year-old brain's interaction with wilderness. As a species, we have devised ways of domesticating natural systems, and while this has caused great harm to the natural world, it has also provided us with a foundation for great hope. We have, within our mind, an evolutionary history of relating well with other species, to particular landscapes, and to one another. We are well suited to engage the natural world as a full cohabitant, and our cultural development does not have to devour wilderness; one needn't come at the expense of the other. Hope is within us, it spreads out over both land and memory in those places we call home. Bear Creek, as it trickles around smooth rock and hauls along small bits of upstream earth, is a reminder that if I get to know its persistent path within the context of homeland, it makes ecological sense, and therefore I can see it in its rightful sense.

NOW MORE GEESE. In a moment they are high overhead, moving en masse almost directly south following a map that is invisible to me. Breathing shallowly, I watch them, arms hanging limp from the sleeves of my tattered cotton jacket. My head swivels as if it were a smooth iron ball in a socket. Then they are gone, and only the valley wind moving across my weather-beaten face seems real.

During my early months here, I felt utterly misplaced. I feared I was without direction, adrift both intellectually and emotionally. Looking back on those cold and closed-in winter months, I was comforted by the writings of Thoreau, Muir, Weil, Gary Snyder, and Wendell Berry. Others like Terry Tempest-Williams, Rudy Weib, Gretel Erlich, and Thomas Merton impressed me as masters of putting their fingers on the deep connections between people and their places. They seemed able to measure moments in individual breaths, to ground thought in firm earth, to wash souls with going-by river water. From them, I learned to hold still and listen deeply, to memorize the Alsek wind even as it relentlessly threw itself against my cabin walls and tried to roll back its red tin roof.

There were many nights I did not sleep well. I would wake feeling tired, disappointed with the pace of my writing, overwhelmed by the enormity of my research. I became obsessed with small bits of information as my unconscious struggled to find suitable locations to park them in a mind already overloaded with cultural and genetic notions. My tonic was always to dig deeper, read more, seek out others who have grappled with similar uncertainty. I was a hopeless theorizing drunk, unable to break free of my own rational maze. Why did I choose this path? Where would I find the courage to take my own thoughts seriously? How would I stand up to this place, the strangeness of a boreal forest, rivers running through a landscape I did not know and therefore could not fully imagine? The rivers in my memory were other rivers, cutting through a different me. But then, after building a fire in the wood stove and tipping my coffee cup a time or two, I regained some sense of possibility. My dog would sigh in his familiar way, or the wind would resonate just right, and I would be back home. My eyes would scan a known landscape, one familiar and full of promise. I would think of my father, Colorado geese, and an old story or two.

On some mornings, standing in fresh silver snow, I watched ravens roll and tuck into a wind so strong it prevented them from flying south into the valley. Hooded in a hat made of moose hide and lynx fur, I would stare up at their lofty black bodies, wondering if there was any truth to be gleaned from their nimble passage through the heavy October sky. Would I find there a ribbon of thought that could stand the same scrutiny to which we subject religion, art, and evolution? I wanted, through the raven's eyes, to see clear of earth's October breath and clear of my intellectual desperation. I longed to be able to call these dark birds into some sort of emotional and intellectual collaboration.

Two hundred yards south of my cabin, Bear Creek weaves its way through tall stands of poplar and spruce into the Alsek valley, where it meets the Dezadeash River. Together they join the torrid Alsek River, and in thirty miles, these thunderous rivers join a third — "Raven's River," the voluminous Tatshenshini. Much further south, this fresh water meets the salty water of the Gulf of Alaska. It is hard to imagine Bear Creek water being much different from water flowing into the Gulf. And is some ways it is not. Creeks move into rivers then into oceans, but sitting by each stream of water is different. I can wrap my mind around Bear Creek. In its smooth flow, I watch a poplar leaf gently curl itself around each small stone. Each breath I take is calm. The Alsek and the Tatshenshini, on the other hand, require real effort. They steal one's breath and splinter consciousness. In Turnback Canyon, the narrow funnel through which the Alsek is forced, one can almost feel the intensity of the two huge tectonic plates that jammed together during the last million years, creating the tremendous pressure that caused earthquakes, volcanoes and ultimately these great chains of mountains.

The sound of these far-north rivers is like none to which I have ever listened. It is water flowing, as Norman Maclean suggested of his great river, from the "basement of time." In this water I hear very old music and the language of legends. I remember sitting one February afternoon along the frozen overflow of Bear Creek a mile or so northeast of where it slides into the Alsek River. Deep in the creek I heard a story of surging water, of moose being swept swirling downstream, of children being violently severed from their homes. Around 1850, the glacial dam that held Lake Champagne broke. A volume of water sixty times that of the Amazon River was released, destroying the entire village of Kaskawulsh, which had been wedged precariously at the confluence of the Alsek and the Tatshenshini. In this water went village, land, and life. Ended were the many journeys that had brought these people to their place. Gone were the whimsy of children and the knowledge of the old. What did not go was what I heard that February afternoon: this place timelessly moving on, the crafting of new river channels, new places for children to make memory.

Stories are held within this northern landscape, to be heard again and again in its rivers. I hear another in the distant and dying howl of a lone wolf that I imagine wandering deep in the Alsek valley along the moonlit ridge above Summit Creek. I can forsee a time in which this howl may be for a mate no longer of this earth. Alone, and in search of some other living wolf, it moves, stalks, yellow eyes focusing intently on the grey light of the valley floor. Breathing very cold arctic air into its lungs, it is unaware of the utterly devastating fact that it is the last wolf. Desperation overwhelms me and, feeling heavy, overtaken by guilt-ridden humanness, I sink into a sympathetic natural stupor. I am keenly aware of the direct link between my unsustainable way of living and the death of wolves. No matter how intellectually or technologically clever I become, it will not be enough to save these wild creatures. In order to fully understand my place in the natural order of things, I must search out some other wisdom. It has been my hope I could find it here, as a journeyman in the broad and solitary expanse of northern Canada — as a pilgrim in search of the relationship between one's ability to be wise and the wilderness through which one travels.

On winter mornings, before first light, I step out onto my front deck. Under my weight it pops in the deep cold.

The sound cracks against the iced-over hillside that folds immediately behind the cabin. As I gather a load of spruce and poplar kindling in my arms, I become aware that I do not hear another sound. Above me, stars arch from atop the Auriols to the distant boreal forest off to the southwest. Were it not for dense stands of spruce towering over my cabin, I could, even in this dim morning light, see to the Ruby Range rising round and humpy to the east. Silence has become the medium of my solitude, and I delight in it as the context for the mystery here in the complex environment that surrounds me. It has served me as well, as a mirror of truth, and on one solitary morning it became instantly clear to me that I could love this valley. I always suspected there was a place where I could feel the feathery touch of winter snow or hear summer rain falling on a shop-worn tin roof creating a rhythm to which I could compose a new beginning.

If one listens to a place long enough, it begins to sound a warm and fluid welcome. I heard it when there was no other sound in this valley except for the coming-down spring rain. I acknowledged it as I would a long note held in a wolf's silver throat. Hearing the rain, I joined it. It was me coming down on the tin roof, running down each corrugation, falling from the worn-tin lip and plunking onto dank earth, evaporating into still air. I realized that this cabin is only a part of home, my stories only a small part of what it means to stay for a while. But this rain is everything, and it has trickled me down into a most ancient place.

This fall I went for a walk into the valley. Finding flat ground just before sun-fall, I sat with my spine as straight as I could. I was surely the tallest object in any direction.

Thinking that, I arched and sat all the straighter. To the south, winds sliced at the Auriol Range pulling a white band of early snow into the blue sky. High above me, a raven artfully tossed itself into the wind. It disappeared between gauze-like fingers of cloud that bent down then flipped upward as if introducing a performance in which all the actors wore thin delicate slippers.

Leaving the valley was as easy as turning around. Lichen, which had cushioned each footstep, sprung restored, and yellow-red leaves from this fall's poplars crawled back into remaining depressions. The whisper of Kaskawulsh Creek finished any statements I may have intended, and I returned to my cabin thinking that, when the world goes on without me, I will know I was here and I was the tallest. Then snow fell, pulling evening light onto these mountains, and there remained no visible record of my walking there.

Long after the sun had gone down, I sat on a white mound of snow that had covered the old dry grass behind my cabin. I listened to the sound of my breathing. The earth turned and, on its axis, tilted a bit to the north. As wind from deep in the Alsek valley rushed over me, pushing me into a tight ball, I heard the sound of geese. My father died alone last November so very far from here. I reached out my hand and touched the small cairn under which I sprinkled his ashes, and I whispered to him in the voice of a journeyman. The language between us is that of geese. It speaks of time and memory. It can be heard in the rivers and it travels on wings that carry the journeyman home and back again.

The Contributors

Philip Adams lived and worked in the Yukon from 1982 to 1999. He is a theatre director, dramaturge and playwright who works with new Canadian plays across the country.

Nicole Bauberger is a poet, painter and storyteller. She has been painting in the Yukon the past three summers, most recently in the Tombstone Mountains.

Ivan E. Coyote, born and raised in Whitehorse, is a writer and storyteller, and the author of three books of short stories. Her CD, *You're A Nation*, was released in June 2003.

Norm Easton lives, writes and teaches anthropology in Whitehorse.

Dean Eyre lives in Whitehorse, where he writes plays and poetry. His latest play, *Blooms*, will be produced by Nakai Theatre in the fall of 2003. He is editor-in-chief of *Out of Service* magazine.

Patti Fraser is a writer, director, and creator for digital media and the theatre. She is currently co-creating a multi-media performance piece for youth. She lives in Vancouver.

Liz Gontard is a writer and editor living in Whitehorse. She is working now on a novella set in Canada and Indonesia.

Michael Hale is a Whitehorse journalist, playwright and poet.

Gregory Heming, poet and essayist, is also the director of the International Symposium on Wisdom and Wilderness in Haines Junction, Yukon.

Graham McDonald is a writer and mediator who lives in Whitehorse.

Roy Ness is a writer, gardener and performer living near Whitehorse. His radio commentaries are heard throughout the North.

Yvette Nolan writes plays, essays, and fiction. She currently serves as the artistic director of Native Earth in Toronto.

Al Pope has written for journals, anthologies, newspapers, and magazines, as well as for radio and the stage. His first novel, *Overflow*, is scheduled for publication with Turnstone Press in 2004.

Michael Reynolds' poetry has been published in *The Fiddlehead*, *The Malahat Review, Grain* and *ICE-FLOE*. He is co-editor of poetry for *Out of Service* magazine.

Tory Russell lives in Whitehorse where she is grateful to work at a Long Term Care facility.

Brenda Schmidt's first book of poetry, *A Haunting Sun*, was published by Thistledown Press in 2001. The poems in this volume are from her new manuscript, *More Than Three Feet of Ice*, which won the 2003 Alfred G. Bailey Prize.

Jerome Stueart is most recently from Texas, but now lives in Whitehorse. A college teacher and part-time cartoonist, he has published in *Out of Service*, *ICE-FLOE* and other journals.